BACK TO
LOVE

SERENDIPITY BOOK TWO

BACK TO
LOVE

KT BOND

4 Horsemen
Publications, Inc.

Back to Love
Serendipity Series Book 2
Copyright © 2022 KT Bond. All rights reserved.

4 Horsemen
Publications, Inc.

4 Horsemen Publications, Inc.
1497 Main St. Suite 169
Dunedin, FL 34698
4horsemenpublications.com
info@4horsemenpublications.com

Cover by Ron Perry Graphic Design, rperrydesign.com
Typesetting by Autumn Skye
Editor CI Stearns

Library of Congress Control Number: 2022932811

Print ISBN: 978-1-64450-564-9
Ebook ISBN: 978-1-64450-563-2
Audio ISBN: 978-1-64450-562-5

DEDICATION

To my big brother, Lloyd—may he rest in peace—
who made England a beloved place. I miss him
more than I can say.

ACKNOWLEDGMENTS

I would never have made it through this second
novel in the series without Linda. I struggled
to get the words out, and to get them out in the
best order that I could. But Linda had my back,
cajoling and supporting me through serious writer's block.

My brother Lloyd—God rest his soul!—was
front and center in my mind every time I had to
research something uniquely English for this story.
Thanks to his love for people and travel, I fell in
love on my last visit in 2019 with places I may
never have visited if he hadn't taken me there. He
brought the towns, the pubs, and bowling greens
to life for me. He made my Anglophilic heart swell
with real love for cities and towns like London,
Birmingham, Lichfield, and Loughborough in
England, and Rhyl in Wales.

And as always, my thanks to Ron, whose
covers are just beautiful, and whose help in getting the book out is always prompt and efficient.

TABLE OF CONTENTS

CHAPTER 1

N iall McLaren slid his sweaty palms over his jacket, irritated with himself for being nervous. This was a first for him. He passed his hand over his impeccably groomed dark hair and hoped that whatever dampness remained on his palms would transfer itself to his tresses. Dressed in a dark gray suit with a white silk dress shirt open at the collar and polished gray loafers, he knew he looked more than presentable enough to pass muster when he saw Karen Mullings again. It wasn't his appearance that had him anxious. It was her reaction to seeing him again that had his heart rate speeding up as he pressed the doorbell.

The first time he'd seen her in the pub a few weeks earlier, he'd been intrigued by the cool, sophisticated air that she'd exuded, and he hadn't been especially concerned by the fact that she was with an older guy. They seemed friendly enough, if the shared smiles and earnest conversation he had observed were anything to go by. But they hadn't seemed to be a couple in the traditional sense, though he thought he read interest in the guy's expression, which didn't surprise him, given how attractive Karen was. He wasn't quite able to read hers, however, so when she showed up the next night alone, he'd taken a chance. What was the worst that could happen? She'd send him packing and he could live with that.

Now, as he rang the doorbell, he knew instinctively that whatever Karen's first response to seeing him again was, it would set the tone for all future contact between them. Eventually, he wanted that contact to be the kind he knew she would never allow him to have if she didn't feel the same interest that he did. Taking a deep, calming breath, he waited for the door to open. When it did, the woman he'd been unable to forget stood before him wearing a silk dress, knee length and clinging to her every curve. Her kitten-heeled sandals were white and strappy, her jewelry understated, her makeup barely there. He was speechless with nerves and thoroughly annoyed with himself.

"Hi! Come in!" Karen said.

Niall stepped inside, finding his voice at last. "Thank you. It's good to see you again."

He was aiming for cool and nonchalant; it would never do for her to see how eager he was feeling until he could be sure of her. Inhaling her fragrance, he observed Karen regarding him with no more than a friendly eye. He sighed inwardly then, knowing at once that he had no chance with her. All the time he'd spent thinking about her since their first meeting had been wasted. Dammit!

She was as alluring as ever but also just as elusive as the first time they'd met. He observed it in her smile, even as she walked ahead of him into the living room. She was friendly, and her eyes were warm, but that was all. Looking around him, he assumed this was going to be a small party, as the space was intimate. How the hell was he going to handle being around her when she so obviously didn't want anything like what he would have liked with her? What a cock-up this was turning out to be!

And then a small, curvy woman in a little black dress walked into the room and his brain sputtered. He knew Karen was speaking to him, but he couldn't focus for a moment. It felt as though all the air in the room had been sucked out, and he needed to hold his breath until oxygen was restored.

"Niall?" Karen's concerned voice finally penetrated his haze, and he cleared his throat before answering.

"Sorry," he said but could find nothing to add to explain his lapse in concentration.

Karen studied him for a second and the small smile she allowed to purse her lips made him cringe. Bloody hell! She knew what had happened and why and was highly entertained by it. But thankfully she said nothing, merely introduced her friend.

"Toni, meet Niall McLaren. Niall, my friend Antonia Larson."

Niall found himself a little annoyed with Karen for finding her friend amusing as they both watched Toni trip over her feet. There was nothing funny in it. He reined in the impulse to reach out and steady her before she tumbled to the floor off the very high stilettos she was wearing. She righted herself without his assistance while he marveled at how he had gone from hoping Karen would return his interest to wishing her to be anywhere but there while he filled his gaze with the woman who had captivated him completely as soon as she walked into the room. That must make him some kind of an arsehole, but he didn't care just then.

"Good evening, Ms. Larson," he said, extending his hand and waiting almost impatiently for her to touch him.

She was a small woman, shorter than Karen but just as curvy, her complexion a sandy tan color, though it wasn't the coppery kind that indiscriminate sunworshippers and spray-tan users had. That probably meant she was of mixed heritage. He wanted to touch her skin, which looked like it might feel silky beneath his fingertips. Pulling back on those thoughts, he focused on her words.

"It's just Toni, Mr. McLaren," she said, and her voice sent shivers over him, like warning shots over the bow of a ship. "It's a pleasure to meet you."

She tilted her head a little and studied him, and he knew what she saw. He was a big man, tall and wide, with no surplus fat anywhere on him. He was six inches over six feet, with full lips that curled up at the corners when he smiled.

He'd been told often enough how his eyes twinkled when he was amused, and that women found the cleft in his chin and his broad shoulders and bulging biceps endlessly appealing. He fought against the hope that Toni would be one of those women.

"My pleasure as well. And please, call me Niall," he replied, breaking the spell they both seemed to be caught in.

And so had begun what turned out to be an even better evening than Niall had been anticipating. The way he and Toni seemed to flow together like two tributaries heading to the same river's mouth was a great surprise to him, especially as whatever attraction he had felt for Karen had dissipated like mist in sunshine. While he wasn't a shy man by any stretch of the imagination, he wasn't a player, either, though Karen might be forgiven for thinking he was based on his about-face this evening.

It was obvious that something powerful had passed between him and Toni, and he was at once enchanted by and concerned about it. He really wasn't in a position to start anything with anyone, but he also knew he wouldn't stop whatever was going to happen between him and this woman he had just met. Not even his first contact with Karen had been this intense. His gut told him this was a big deal and he shouldn't muck it up.

By the time the party ended, Niall was sure everyone had noticed each time he and Toni had ended up in some quiet corner by themselves. Had they seen how deeply he had looked into her eyes or how close they had come to kissing each other that last time? He had never been a particularly possessive man, preferring to keep his dalliances light. He should have known Fate had something in store for him when he met Karen because the pull he had felt toward her had been unexpectedly acute. It just hadn't occurred to him that she had merely been a means to a different end. Why would it? That had never happened before.

Now it was time to leave, and he freely admitted that he didn't want to go anywhere. He assumed that Karen was staying with her friend, but he wanted her gone. Maybe he could put her up in a hotel... He let the thought go with a soft chuckle. He was really losing his mind if he wanted to get rid of the first woman he'd been interested in so he could get with the second woman he was even more fascinated by.

"What's so funny?" Toni had heard his chuckle.

There was no way he was telling her where he had gone in his head. "Nothing. I had a good time this evening. Thank you for allowing Karen to invite me."

He watched as her cheeks grew warm, and he wondered what she was thinking. "I'm glad you accepted her invitation." She smiled and added, biting her bottom lip, "She's right about you, you know? You're definitely a chick magnet."

He didn't react to her words. Truth be told, he barely heard them because he was consumed by the desire to suck that lip into his mouth, especially when she moistened it with the tip of her tongue. He blinked to get himself back under control before he let his mind wander too far off the appropriate track for a first meeting. What he needed was more time with her. But how was he to get it?

"May I call you sometime?" he asked baldly. Finesse wasn't something he could manage when his brain was turning to mush. "Here's my number." He had come prepared this time and pulled one of his business cards out of his wallet and handed it to her. "In case you ever need me, this has all the ways to find me," he told her. "You can call my cell phone any time."

He didn't have time to register the thought that this would be the first time he had ever given his business card to anyone for whom he was not going to be working because she smiled at him again and his heart tripped over itself. The last time he had felt anything like this, or been so out of control, he had barely been out of his teens. What the hell was happening to him? He inhaled deeply, trying to slow his heartbeats and wrestle back control over his breathing.

"Thank you."

Quietly spoken words, but coupled with the look in her eyes, they were potent. He would do anything she asked of him at this point, so when she said, "Give me your cell phone," he handed it over like an obedient servant. Maybe she was adding her number to his contact list. He didn't really care just then. He just desperately wanted to kiss her.

He could hear Karen returning to the living room—when had she left it?—and she was clearly trying to be as loud as possible so they would hear her. She still managed to interrupt their last tender moment at the door when Niall bent his head to kiss Toni's cheek. He lingered there before raising his head.

"You have no idea how much I want to kiss you someplace less chaste," he whispered in her ear. "But I think we would both prefer that there's no audience for that, hmm?"

Toni smiled and blushed as Karen cleared her throat and walked fully into the room. Neither of them moved, and Niall didn't care about what she might have seen. If nothing else proved Karen had definitely not been the one for him, his current indifference to her seeing him with another woman ably illustrated the point to anyone who cared. He didn't.

"I know this isn't my place, Toni, but I'm ready for some zzz's."

Karen chuckled as she said it, and he assumed that Toni would understand whatever the code was in that comment. He didn't think Karen was being rude, and when Toni looked over at her friend before looking back up at him, he knew he was right.

She chuckled as she said, "You'd better go, Niall. This is Karen's sleeping quarters!"

Niall turned to look at Karen, his black eyes twinkling with understanding and amusement.

"It was good to see you again," he said, walking back to grip her hand in both of his. "And I have a feeling we'll be seeing a lot more of each other from now on."

He hoped she would see his gratitude and understand his unspoken meaning in the smile he slanted at her, and when she returned it as she watched him turn back to leave, he knew she did.

"Goodnight, beautiful," he said to Toni, resisting the urge to kiss her again. "Sweet dreams."

"Goodnight, Niall."

He didn't fall asleep quickly that night, his mind whirling as he went over every aspect of his evening, from the moment he saw Toni approach to their kiss goodnight. He had been bold and she had not refused him. He smiled as he remembered the conversation where they talked about what they did for work.

"I'm a social worker at Hope House," she'd told him, chuckling when he asked if she was also a writer. "Karen is the one with the fertile imagination. I'm just her happy sidekick, willing to read anything she writes." She had eyed him quizzically. "And what do you do?"

"I'm in law enforcement, but no, I'm not a policeman." He answered the question everyone asked when he told them what he did for a living.

Her eyes widened but she made no further comment and excused herself when the birthday girl called her. He had followed her progress around the room, waiting for the next moment when he could snag her attention for himself again. Her living room was spacious, the earth tones of the furniture, walls, and flooring giving it a warm appeal. And with the soft lights and the music, it was even more welcoming.

He had managed to get one dance with her, and he would have sworn that sparks literally flew between them as they held each other. He had deliberately chosen the slow dance because he had an overwhelming need to touch her for more than an accidental moment. And by the time the number ended, he knew he wanted to be with her for more than a few minutes at a party with strangers.

By the time he fell into a fitful slumber, he had decided to invite both Toni and Karen out for the day. The text message from his best friend reminding him of the backyard party he was hosting at his home the next day was the perfect excuse for more Toni time. It would be a good, safe, fun way to spend a few hours with the woman he was obsessing over without slighting Karen. In the company of others, he would retain more control, and they could get to know each other a little better.

CHAPTER 2

Niall was up with the four-o'clock doves—way too early, though nothing unusual for him —the morning after the birthday party he'd gone to thinking he might score with Karen Mullings. His busy mind wouldn't let him stay asleep, so he sent Toni a text message, delaying sending it until he felt like she'd be awake, at least. Jacob Walker, Niall's friend and business partner, lived almost an hour away, and Niall thought a nice day in the suburbs would be a pleasant way to spend a Sunday.

[Niall: Good morning. This is Niall. Are you and Karen busy today? Would you like to spend the day with me?]

He didn't try to finesse the message. He was too wired by unusual insecurity to waste the effort. He put the phone down on the kitchen counter and brewed tea for something to do while he waited none too patiently for a reply. He was sipping his first cup when the phone vibrated. Reaching for it, he read the message with indescribable glee.

[Toni: Good morning to you, too, Niall. Thanks for asking, and no, we don't have any plans so we'd be delighted to spend the day with you.]

He didn't care that a huge grin split his face at her response. He hadn't thought through what he'd do if she refused, so he wasn't too proud to be relieved that she hadn't.

[Niall: I'll pick you up at ten.]

That would give them both enough time to have a good breakfast and get ready for the day.

[Toni: Dress code?] She sent back the question a second later.

[Niall: Casual's good.]

He showered and changed into dark jeans and a light blue Polo shirt. Then he made himself a quick breakfast, doing his best not to hurry over the eggs and sausages with toast, sipping his tea slowly, enjoying the flavors and feeling of fullness when he was done. He refused to act like an over-eager schoolboy, rushing to get the girl before she changed her mind. Forty was old enough to know how to be grown up.

He spent the entire drive thinking back on the moments he'd spent in Toni's company the evening before. She was the perfect hostess, so those moments had been few, but they'd been enough to impress him with her beauty and poise as she'd moved from group to group, welcoming her guests and making them feel comfortable. He'd watched her with Rory, the guy who had come as her plus one, and read enough of the energy between them to know he had nothing to worry about from that end.

He'd seen how she'd set up Rory with Chrissy, the guest of honor, and he'd also noticed how the birthday girl had done a poor job of hiding her own interest in Rory. Toni and Karen were like two peas in a pod with the way they flowed together. That was a deep friendship, he realized, and it made him smile to know the two women he liked had each other's back. People watching was fun when it wasn't connected to his work, and last night there'd been enough opportunities to watch Toni without appearing to do so.

How would it go today? As far as he was concerned, Karen would be just the buffer they needed between them because the chemistry had been simmering all evening, and he was in no less an aroused state now than he'd been when he'd left Toni's flat the night before. He could only hope that she still felt the connection between them as sharply as he did.

Toni curled up in the corner of the sofa, hugging her knees that she had drawn up to her chest. Karen was reclining with the blankets drawn up around her.

"How do you feel about a day in the country?" she asked after she hung up from the call she'd just received from Niall.

"Sounds like fun. Was that Niall?"

Toni bore her friend's teasing grin. She had only ever responded to another man so immediately once before and that had not ended well. She knew she should be cautious of the big man whom she'd only met the previous evening, but there was just something about him that drew her like an ant to sugar.

"He's invited you, too, so don't go jumping to conclusions, missy. He could just be trying to decide which one of us he wants..."

Karen shook her head. "Please! Don't even go there, Toni. Anyone with half an eye could see how the two of you were dancing around each other last night."

Toni searched her friend's face. Niall had hit on her in a pub, if Karen was to be believed, and he'd come to the party the night before as her date. Was she angry that he seemed to have switched gears? Should Toni not have accepted the invitation for the two of them? What if Karen didn't want to spend any more time with either of them because she was upset with them both?

She must have waited too long to respond because Karen said again, "If you'd rather I didn't go, that's fine. I can always catch up on my sleep."

"No," Toni hastened to reassure her. "That's the last thing I want. I mean, I don't really know this guy any better than you do, right? So, it's best if we go together, so we can have each other's back in case of anything happening."

"Does he scare you? If you don't trust him, you shouldn't go. Call him back and say something's come up. Make something up... I'm throwing up. It's an emergency, so you're taking me to A&E. Your parents arrived unexpectedly and are on their way over..."

Toni laughed. "When are you going to finish that novel you started? Because you've certainly got stories to tell!"

"Well, I am a writer, yes? It's what I do... I invent truths for my fiction. Oh, the irony!"

They both collapsed in laughter again before Toni sobered enough to answer her friend's question. "He doesn't scare me. He's got a really strong caring vibe, you know? I'm sure you felt it, right alongside that seductive one. But I think if he meant me harm, he wouldn't have invited you along."

"Or he could be using me to lull you into a false sense of security before he pounces when I'm back in Birmingham."

They looked at each other again for a split second before bursting into giggles again. Toni jumped up suddenly, saying, "Wait a sec! He slipped me his business card last night. Let's see what he does for a living. That might help us stop making up fantastic stories about him."

When she returned, she was clutching a black matte business card in her hand.

"It says here," she cleared her throat, "Niall McLaren, Senior Investigator, M & W Investigations."

"So he's a private detective?"

Toni shrugged. "Sounds like it."

Karen sighed. "Well, at least we can be sure if anything bad happens, he'll probably be able to protect us."

Toni chuckled. "Do you remember the size of him, girl? He looks like he could bench press you. I'm not worried about him taking care of us."

Come to think of it, she wasn't worried about him at all. But there was nothing wrong with considering every possibility. He was still an unknown entity, no matter how hot the sparks were that had arced between them the night before. She was glad Karen was going with her. She refused to let uncertainty or fear stop her from having a good time, and she knew with her friend there, she could relax.

"What time is he coming? I hope we have time for breakfast because I'm starving."

As if to demonstrate the truth of her words, Karen's stomach rumbled. More laughter followed and they got off the sofa and went to get breakfast. Toni ate most of the omelet that Karen made for her, but she could only handle one slice of toast, and she took the rest of her coffee back to the bedroom with her. She was feeling too fluttery, almost nervous, and she didn't want to overindulge and heave the food she'd just eaten.

Deciding what to wear for a day in the country was a lot harder than she had thought it would be, and Toni knew that had a lot to do with the fact that she wanted to impress Niall. That in itself should have upset her. She wasn't that woman, not after Randy. She didn't dress to please anyone but herself, so why she was fretting over what would look good to him now was a mystery.

She rushed through her shower, scented her body with lotion and perfume, and picked up her now cold coffee to finish it. She loved coffee, hot or cold, so she didn't mind it. Reaching for the white top she'd chosen to wear with the black jeans she'd pulled out, she tripped over the slippers she'd kicked off, spilling coffee all over her hand, the blouse, and the slippers at her feet.

"Dammit!" she growled in frustration. Now she'd have to find something else to wear.

"Everything okay in there?" Karen's voice sounded outside her door.

"Yeah. I just need to change my outfit. Wanna come help me? It took me long enough to choose the first outfit!"

Her aggravation sounded in her voice as her friend walked in and looked at the mess of clothing on her bed.

"Well, unless you're planning to pull out the iron, you'll have to choose something that's not lying on your bed," Karen pointed out.

Toni sighed. She was going to be the reason they were late because why would Fate help her make a good first impression? She followed Karen into the closet and waited. Her friend was very practical, and she knew she could trust her to make a quick and correct decision.

"How about this?"

Karen held up a red three-quarter-sleeved summer sweater under which hung a soft pink shell. That might work, though not with the white shoes. She nodded.

"It could work if I changed the shoes," she said.

Karen hung it on the back of the closet door. "We only have time for one more outfit change," she informed Toni, "before you'll be very late."

Karen turned back to the clothes hanging in front of her and pulled out the new royal blue calf-length jumpsuit that Toni had bought but never worn. It looked good on her, accentuating all her curves, and it would still go well with the footwear she'd chosen. Thank God for small mercies.

"Hurry up and finish getting ready. I'll let him in when he gets here."

"Lifesaver!" Toni exclaimed, blowing her friend a kiss. "I'll dance at your wedding."

Karen's chuckles followed her out of the room, and Toni spared a moment to clean up the mess made by the coffee on the carpet and dumped the soiled shirt in the hamper before getting dressed. She heard the buzzer, heard first Karen's voice, then Niall's and cast a final look over her lightly made-up face and upswept hair before exiting the room on suddenly shaky legs. She needed to get a grip before she went out to meet Niall, or she'd be off-kilter for the rest of the day, and that wasn't something she was prepared to be. He was just a man... a very charismatic, attractive, sexy-as-sin man, but still just a man for all that.

Steadying her breathing, she slung the white slouch bag over her shoulder and walked out confidently, the sight of him in his jeans and Polo shirt somehow easing her nerves, so that her smile was genuine, not forced. His smile in return made her belly flutter but in a good way. Maybe this was a sign that the day would go well. She'd keep her fingers crossed and hope for the best.

When Niall arrived back at Toni's flat, his usual cheerful persona firmly in place, he waited a few minutes before ringing her buzzer. Karen answered the door, looking delightful in black pedal pushers and a bright white sleeveless cotton blouse. She looked cool and relaxed, and her smile was warm as she let him into the flat.

"Good morning. Toni's almost ready," she said.

"Morning, lovely lady. How are you this morning?"

"I'm fine. Thanks for asking. Looking forward to a day in the country. Is it far, where we're going?"

Niall smiled. He knew what Karen was doing and he wished he could hug her without sending any mixed signals. She didn't want him to be upset that Toni was late, so she was doing her best to distract him. He followed where she led him.

"It's about an hour away. I think you'll both enjoy it."

Toni appeared just then, her hair pinned up on top of her head, her body clad in a sleeveless royal blue jumpsuit. The outfit clung to every curve and line of her body, ending at mid-calf. He let his eyes rove down to her feet. She was wearing white slip-on canvas shoes and no socks. Between the soft muscular curve of her calves and her narrow ankles, he found himself unexpectedly turned on even more.

She walked over to him with a welcoming smile. "Good morning. Sorry I'm late. I had a wardrobe mishap and had to change outfits."

Niall winked at her. "Good morning. I'm not complaining. You look beautiful."

"Thank you." She lowered her eyes, and Niall knew if she were any fairer, he would see the blush her skin tone was hiding.

"Ready?" The question felt superfluous, but he felt he needed to ask anyway. When she nodded, he went on. "Well, then, let's get going."

The party had already started when they arrived, and Niall introduced Toni and Karen as his friends, but he knew the guys were watching him. And he knew they wouldn't miss the heated regard that he often pinned on Toni. He did his best to be circumspect throughout the afternoon, but he knew he hadn't managed to hide his interest when Jake, his best friend and business partner, cornered him at the grill. He and Jake had become friends while they were still in the military, both assigned to a joint special forces operation.

"So, you finally found a woman you don't want to run screaming away from, eh?"

"What makes you say that?" He would try to play it off if he could.

Jake had clearly noticed the signs of possessiveness in Niall's behavior that he had done his best to disguise all afternoon. The thought of any of his mates making a play for Toni bothered him more than he was ready to admit to anyone, even to his best friend. He'd tried to play it off, but Jake saw right through his bullshit.

"Don't try to kid a kidder," he said, smirking at Niall.

"I brought two women with me today."

Niall tried a different tactic, hoping to deflect his friend's attention away from his reactions to Toni, but he knew it was likely to be a fruitless effort. Jake rolled his eyes and scoffed.

"Really, dude? Is this how you wanna play this?"

Jake's American accent usually became much more pronounced when he was exasperated or angry. Clearly, Niall was getting on his last nerve, as he would no doubt say if pushed to extremes.

"I only met them recently," he said again. "In fact, I only met Toni yesterday."

"And yet, she's here today, and you can't keep your eyes off her. So, how about we cycle back to my original question which, in case you didn't understand, I'll rephrase. Do you like this woman? Oh, and before you answer, please consider how often you've bored holes into her with your eyes, how often she's returned the favor, and how pissed you get every time one of the other guys so much as looks at her."

Niall sighed. It really was no use denying any of Jake's rather astute observations. The man was a top investigator in the firm, and he was damned good at what he did. Niall's current discomfiture was a testament to how handily Jake had observed and interpreted his behavior.

"She's a beautiful woman," he commented.

Jake snorted. "So's the other woman... Karen, right? She's not even remotely unattractive, and you couldn't care less about her. So, spare me the obvious answer. It's about more than how she looks. And the very fact that you either can't figure out how to explain it or are—wonder of wonders!— afraid to name it, tells me that this woman has already got you tied up in knots."

And that was no lie. Niall sighed again. "Look, I don't know what it is, but..." He paused, trying to gather his thoughts. "Something about her just calls to me. It's bizarre."

"It's normal," Jake answered in amusement.

"How would you know, Mr. Afraid-to-Commit?" Niall could dish it as well as the next man.

"It's an abundance of caution not fear that keeps me single," Jake retorted. "If I ever decide to commit, you can bet your life she'll be bulletproof."

Niall laughed loud enough to cause a few pairs of eyes to swing in their direction.

"So you're on the hunt for the perfect woman, eh? Good luck with that. Let me know when you find her."

"Don't think you've distracted me from the subject of the little woman you're stuck on, but I'll give you some time to wrap your head around the knowledge that you've been hit by the arrow of looooove!"

He dragged out the last word and made a thumping noise with his lips as if to indicate an arrow hitting its target. They both laughed, though Niall felt unease well up at his friend's use of "love" to describe his attraction to Toni. He hadn't thought he would ever fall in love. Could this thing with Toni prove him wrong and fill that void? It was much too early to decide that, but he didn't squelch the spurt of hope that rose inside him at the idea. Maybe he wasn't a lost cause after all.

CHAPTER 3

N iall didn't manage to kiss Toni goodnight in the way he wanted to when he took her and Karen back to her flat later that night. He felt a spurt of annoyance that he couldn't lay one on her because Karen was still in the car. This must really be some kind of personal playboy record he was setting because not long ago, Karen had been the one he'd been interested in cozying up to. He sighed inwardly at the thought as they stepped out of the elevator and walked toward Toni's flat, and his irritation with Karen fizzled when she made herself scarce as soon as he opened the door to the apartment.

He dropped his lips to Toni's cheek as soon as the door closed behind Karen. Thank God Karen was the kind of woman she was. He hadn't sensed even a moment of discomfort from her with having him there, nor did she seem to care that he and Toni were making moon eyes at each other. Moon eyes... that's what Jake had called it. The thought made him smile.

"When I really kiss you properly for the first time," he whispered as he lifted his lips from her cheek, "the earth will move."

He waggled his eyebrows at her, making her laugh, which was what he wanted. Somewhere inside him, a hunger was rising to make her smile, to give her pleasure.

"You're silly, aren't you?" She chuckled with the question.

"I can be. Do you like silly men?"

Another chuckle accompanied her response. "I like men who can be silly without fear."

"When can I see you again, Toni?" The need to be serious weighed on him. "I'll be out of town for a couple of days. Can we make a date for the weekend? We can do anything you want."

She had to know she had options when it came to being with him. He refused to boss her around or make demands without checking in with her.

"I have an event on Saturday evening for my job. It's a black-tie event. Would you like to come as my plus one?"

He didn't care that he was a last-minute thought. They'd only known each other a day so he was flattered that she liked him enough to even think about him. Reining in his excitement, he nodded. "I'd love to be your plus one, thank you. What time shall I pick you up?"

"Seven is good." She paused for a moment, and he watched her face, trying to read the expression on it. "I had a great time today, Niall. Thanks for inviting me."

He leaned in again, drawn to the dewy skin glowing at him and left another heated kiss on each cheek.

"I'm glad." He smiled at her. "I need to go now, Toni. Sweet dreams."

Giving her a salute, he walked away, ignoring the urgent desire to turn around and go back for a proper kiss. Every interaction with her just grew in intensity and as he'd walked back down to his car, he'd tried to sort out the impressions that she had left with him and the emotions that accompanied them.

Toni was a counselor and social worker in a women's shelter called Hope House. She had shared some of her story with him earlier, as they'd both watched his friends gather around Karen to quiz her about the books she wrote. Based on what she'd told him, Toni worked hard at her job, feeling especially connected to the women who were suffering as she had under the fists and bodies of abusive men.

"The organization frowns on us befriending our clients, so I do my best to ensure that they never feel anything from me aside from professional concern and support. I do everything I can to find them supportive friends and encourage them when they find women they can trust."

"It must be hard on you, keeping your distance emotionally," he'd observed, reading her expression.

She'd sighed. "It is, sometimes, especially with the women who are really invested in moving forward but are also really frightened of being found and dragged back to be hurt or possibly killed."

Niall waited, conscious that she wasn't finished with her thoughts.

"None of them know that I share a common history with them."

He'd looked up sharply at that. She'd been abused by her ex? Before he could ask anything, she hurried on, as if she didn't want to answer any questions.

"It isn't their concern, for starters, and it won't help them focus on their own issues if they're commiserating with me over my misfortunes." She looked away from him for a long moment, her eyes seemingly focused on the hedgerows that separated Jake's yard from his neighbor's.

"I escaped and found my way to a safe and happier present, and I know I can't guarantee that for any of them because my life and theirs are different. Best not to encourage comparisons by oversharing, you know?"

He understood completely and new respect and admiration for the woman who was sitting quietly next to him rose in his chest. He wanted to hold her, to make foolish promises he had no business making after such a short acquaintance. He wanted to keep her safe, and he wanted to find the arsehole who had hurt her and finish him off.

Bringing his thoughts back to the present, he looked around him. Hope House had put together a great event, and their fundraiser drew a monied crowd to the intimate space in the central London hotel that she gave him directions to on Saturday. He schmoozed with a couple of lords and ladies, a baron or two, three or four knights of the realm and a host of filthy rich benefactors who helped keep the organization afloat and thriving.

Once again, as he watched her in her element, networking and chatting up the people whose support the shelter needed, his admiration for her grew even more. She never lost her smile, and even when he stepped away to give her room to do her job, he could still feel the warmth of her genuine attention as she listened to the people she was with. He tried his hardest not to react when a few of the men gave her more than a once-over, eyeing her with clear desire and even lust.

He was grateful that she remained unaware of their attention, or that if she did know, she didn't respond to it in any way. He knew he had no right to be jealous, but that knowledge did little to halt the irrational feeling from swelling every time he caught another man's eyes on her. He really needed to get himself in check. This was not normal behavior for him, and he refused to let it become a habit going forward. Toni was her own person, and he was a rational adult, not an immature boy.

After the fundraiser, during which she'd introduced him to many of her colleagues and he had become aware of just how integral a part of the organization she was, he left with even greater respect for her and a need to do for her what she did for others every day. He'd also been aware of all the stares they had been receiving all evening, and as he was taking her home, he asked her about it.

"I don't think I was especially gauche or loud or obnoxious tonight, so why all the attention?

We were being skewered by so many eyes, it's a wonder we're not bleeding right now."

She replied laughingly, "I'm not known for bringing plus ones to these events, except for Karen. I guess people were just surprised that I know someone other than my bestie. And that the someone is male."

An unexpected moment of insecurity needed the answer to the next question he asked. "So, no significant other for a while then?"

She eyed him, amusement but also—strangely—caution in her gaze. "I told you I was divorced seven years ago, remember? So no, no significant other."

Wow! She'd been without a man since her divorce. It hadn't really registered until she'd said it that he wanted to hear her say the words, to ensure that he had a clear field in which to make his play. He had never been lacking in confidence when it came to pursuing women, but Toni was teaching him how deeply he had hidden the insecurity that was probably the reason he hadn't tried for anything serious with anyone before. He was not a fan of this level of self-discovery, but neither was he a coward. He would man up, accept it, and move forward.

This time, his kiss goodnight moved from soft pecks on each perfumed cheek to a sweet press of their lips. He sensed that she might be ready for more, but he wanted to be sure. Something told him she would appreciate him romancing her with sweet kisses and keeping her waiting for the moment when they chose to explore more. He knew he was enjoying the tease, the anticipation, the warmth that enveloped him as he struggled with his own desires.

For their next date, Niall took her to see *Small Island* at the National Theater. He remembered the conversation where she'd told him she had been born in England of a Barbadian father and a Trinidadian mother, so he was sure she would appreciate the show on those grounds, at least. And though he didn't feel a need to impress her, he felt instinctively that she was the kind of woman who appreciated fine art in all its forms.

"I thought you'd enjoy the play, given your West Indian heritage," he told her as they rode the elevator down to his car. "You'll have to let me know if I was right."

The show was superlative, and he loved how she gushed about everything, from the cast— "I knew I recognized the actress who plays Hortense. She's the black nurse in *Call the Midwife*" —to the performances, to the story itself. And he had been lucky because she had read the novel on which the play was based, so she was familiar with it in a way he wasn't.

Afterward, he took her for a late supper, and they dawdled over drinks until closing, talking about the play, about the show she'd refer- enced that he didn't know a thing about but that he promised he'd watch with her the next time he went over for a visit. His heart leapt at the unspoken invitation to spend time with her in her flat. He knew she wasn't thinking along the same lines as he was, that it was more friendly than anything else, but it spoke of her interest in spending time with him, doing things together, even if only as friends.

"Are your parents still in England?" he asked as they sipped their after dinner drinks.

She nodded. "They spend the winters in Barbados and the summers here or traveling. They'll be here for a couple months more before they go down."

"Have you been to their island homes?" he wanted to know next.

"We went all the time when I was young. But I haven't been in a few years." She sounded wistful.

"Why not? Don't you get time off for holidays?"

"Yes, but..." She hesitated and he wondered what she was keeping from him. "I haven't traveled out of the country since the divorce."

He could see she wasn't going to say any more on the subject, and though he wondered why and would ask eventually, he let it go for the moment. He wouldn't spoil their evening by risking dragging up unhappy memories. He wanted her to remember their evening together with pleasure untainted by any sadness. He changed the subject.

"I'd like to take a Caribbean holiday some time. Maybe you can be my guide."

He watched as her eyes lit up and a smile warmed her face. This he could get behind... this sweet, warm, contented woman who looked like she wouldn't mind being his tour guide. He wanted to linger over their last drinks, and he wanted to rush her away to somewhere private so he could take the kisses he wanted and bid her goodnight in the best way he knew how. He restrained himself and managed to hold off until they were once again at her front door.

This time, their parting kiss was everything he could have hoped for ... unrestrained, hopeful, hungry.

She let him in when he said quietly in her ear after gently nipping the lobe,"I think we can take our goodnight kiss to the next level tonight, don't you? I mean, I did knock it out of the park with the play, didn't I? You loved it, which makes it a triumph for me. So, a sort of 'thank you' and 'you're welcome' kiss goodnight?"

She laughed. Another point for Team Niall. "Thank you," she teased before opening to his invading tongue.

He groaned at the sweet taste of her in his mouth, losing himself for a long moment in the feel of her tongue, and the way her body melted against him as they kissed outside her door.

"I hope you had enough of a good time that you'll go out with me again," he whispered in her ear when he let go of her mouth.

"You definitely know how to show a girl a good time, Mr. McLaren," she whispered back, a teasing smile on her lips. "So I wouldn't refuse another invitation."

"Where to next time?"

"I like your surprises. Keep them coming."

It was hard to release her so she could walk into her flat alone, but he was determined to do things right with this woman. At his age, messing up was no longer an option.

"I'll call you, okay? I'm working a case that may take me out of town for a day or two."

"Can't wait." She reached up and brushed his lips lightly once more before slipping inside.

He stayed there until he heard the lock snick into place before he walked away. Romancing a woman was not something he'd ever given much thought to before, but now, as he drove back to his own home, his mind played over all the possibilities. The end game was no longer just to get into Toni's bed. Truth be told, he was quite prepared to wait for that to happen. His main purpose now was to cement their growing friendship, to deepen the bond he felt forming between them. He wanted more from her than a roll in the hay, which shocked him to no end.

A surveillance job would take him away for a week, and he needed to see her one more time before then. His parents expected him for dinner on Sunday, but he could take Toni for a spin before that. He was quite certain that it wasn't time for her to meet his parents, especially as he knew he wasn't ready to meet hers. And since she admitted to not really taking any time for herself, a spin in the country would be a good way for them both to blow away the cobwebs and just enjoy the day.

"I'll be away for a week for work starting tomorrow, and I'd like to see you again. How would you like to go for a drive on Sunday morning?" he asked, when he called her the next day. "I have an evening engagement," he said as his inner voice castigated him for not telling her where he was going, "but I'd like to spend some time with you before."

"I'd like that, thank you." She sounded pleased.

"We can have a picnic lunch somewhere if you like." The idea had only just occurred to him. "We can go to Guildford Castle. You'll love the gardens, and we can picnic by the river."

"That sounds great. Looking forward to it. What do you need me to bring?"

"Nothing. I'll arrange everything and come by to get you by nine."

The next morning, dressed in black jeans and a cream linen button-down shirt, he placed the picnic basket carefully into the boot, making sure he had the wine in its own carrier before he set off. Toni was waiting for him on the sidewalk, wearing a sweet floral sleeveless summer dress and a snazzy wide-brimmed summer hat to match. He got out to help her into the car.

"Good morning. Did you sleep well?"

"Like a baby, thank you. Good morning to you, too." She returned his greeting with a smile.

An hour later, after he parked the car, they walked to the castle and found a lovely spot by the river to settle down. Toni spread the blanket and he placed the basket on top before helping her to sit down. He sprawled next to her on the grass and turned to face her.

"What do you think? We'll wander around the gardens after brunch."

"That sounds fine," she replied with a smile, "but this is truly lovely as well."

He watched her look around her and he tried to see it through her eyes. "Is this your first time coming here?" he asked.

"Yes. Most of my away-from-London pursuits that are not related to my job have been in places other than Guildford. And to be honest, I haven't been on a picnic in ages."

"Well, I'm glad I had the idea, then."

When she chuckled unexpectedly, Niall looked at her curiously. "Share the joke?"

She shook her head, still grinning. "It's really nothing. I was just wondering what those two are arguing about." She pointed to their right, to two older people who were clearly disagreeing about something or other.

"Any ideas?" he wondered, grinning himself.

"Not a one. What do older people argue about when they're supposed to be having fun?"

Niall shrugged. "Who knows? Maybe a disagreement about who forgot the sauce?"

She laughed and he pulled a bunch of grapes from the basket and handed her a few, and they people-watched for a while. To be honest, though, Niall spent more time watching Toni than he spent watching the people around them. The way her cheeks filled when she smiled, the crinkled corners of her eyes as she gazed at the swans and ducks floating by on the river, her quiet composure, the way she didn't try to fill every silence with words... he was finding everything about her completely captivating.

They wandered around the gardens after they ate, and Niall happily stole snapshots of her as she bent to sniff the flowers or spread her arms wide and grinned up at the sunny sky or smiled sweetly at the children who passed by. One little boy, no more than three or four, waved at her as he walked by, his little cheeks round with the sweetest smile. Niall raised his phone and snapped the picture just as Toni blew the child a kiss. They laughed together before his mother smiled at her and they walked away.

Did she want children? She was still young enough that if she found someone with whom she wanted to share the privilege of raising young ones, she could do so. He refused to let the thought that she would find some man who wasn't him to give the gift of children take up any space in his brain. She was with him. That was all there was to it. Nothing else mattered ... for now.

CHAPTER 4

"Jake, do you have any idea how bloody early it is here?" Niall groused as he sat up in bed. Glancing out the window he saw that it was still dark, though the first signs of an approaching dawn, otherwise known as the doves that would have woken him anyway with their mournful songs, had already begun to warm up for their main event.

"Stop whining, Mac," Jake answered good-naturedly, using his nickname for Niall and clearly not even remotely upset at his tone. "You know your ass would have been up anyway. You're the king of stupid o'clock wake-up calls and you know it."

Niall sighed. "What do you want this early?" He didn't feel like conceding any points to his friend, even if Jake was right.

"I thought I spotted our target last night, but by the time I moved to confirm, he'd slipped away."

Wide awake now, Niall ran a hand over his dark hair and released a heavy sigh. They had recently been hired to follow the trail leading to a slippery snake of a man who got his jollies and his wealth from human trafficking and all its attendant sins. Randy Richards had been successfully eluding the authorities for the last year, always managing to stay just out of reach. And even though they had managed to nab some of his henchmen, he was the prize they most wanted.

Which was how Niall's company, M&W Investigations, had ended up being called in to assist with surveillance. They had built a reputation for getting their target, and it was a feather in the company's cap to be asked to participate in this global manhunt, even if only in an unofficial capacity. As a senior partner in the firm and as one of the senior investigators, Niall had taken the job along with Jake, who had gone to Rome following a lead on the suspect.

"What do you need from me?" Niall was all business now.

"Nothing right now. I just needed you to know we lost the slippery shit again." Jake's American drawl held a sharp note of disgust.

Niall sighed in agreement. "We need to stop doing that." He clenched his teeth in frustration that they were so close and yet so far from catching this particular bad guy. The three young people, two girls and a boy, whom they had rescued from his clutches, all now safely housed in secure private facilities, had been an invaluable help in getting as far as they had.

"Yeah, though to be fair, we've only been after him for a couple of weeks now, following the information we've been given. Maybe it's time we did some footwork on our own?"

They'd discussed this before, not wanting to step on any government agency's toes but knowing that sometimes their methods brought faster and better results.

"Let's revisit this when you get back. How soon will that be?" He heard shuffling and wondered where his partner was.

"Flight leaves in an hour, so I'll be there by seven-thirty."

"I'll pick you up."

They ended the call, and Niall got out of bed. His day always started with a workout, no matter where he was, except when he was in active pursuit of a suspect. As he pulled on his running shorts and a t-shirt, he thought about all the work ahead of him. He and Jake would need to review all the notes they'd gathered so far, add in whatever new info Jake had and then figure out a way to get Richards before his next projected auction, which they figured would be sooner rather than later.

What had Richards been doing in Rome? Many of the young women and girls, as well as the boys and young men—because of course he didn't discriminate—were Eastern European and African. And that didn't include all the British citizens that he took. Was he setting up shop in Rome to escape the increased attention in Britain and the States? Interpol already had a file on this man, but they'd need to update them about this latest sighting.

After his five-mile run, he finished his workout routine, showered and was ready to head to the airport. At this time of the morning, he'd be lucky not to hit traffic, so he sent a message to tell Jake he was on his way. His friend would see it when he deplaned. Jake looked exhausted when Niall finally saw him, and he grabbed the overnight bag from him and slung it into the back seat while his friend situated himself in the front.

"Food first?" he asked, turning to look at Jake, whose head lolled against the headrest.

"Nah. I'm bushed. Take me home."

Niall nodded and set off for Jake's place. His friend lived in a two-bedroom cottage with a nice-sized garden behind it. He watched Jake stir as he slowed to a stop outside his home and waited until he opened his eyes.

"How do you do that?" he wondered aloud. "One minute you're sleeping like the dead, the next you're awake and ready to rumble."

Jake sat up, shrugging and rubbing a hand over his face before yawning widely. "I dunno. My body must be hot-wired to the apartment."

He reached back for his duffel and opened the door. "When do you need me in the office?"

"That depends. How much sleep do you need?"

Jake chuckled. "More than there's time for. I'll come in after lunch."

Niall watched his friend's tall, lanky body until it disappeared through the front entrance to his home before he drove off, heading to the corporate offices where they did much of their work when they weren't on assignment. His father was already there, and after pouring himself a cup of tea that the office assistant had miraculously just brewed for his arrival, he walked into his father's office, knocking briefly more to announce his presence than to request permission to enter.

"Morning, son. Jake back safely?"

Alistair McLaren looked twenty years younger than his seventy-five years, as dashing and debonair as he looked when he'd first started the company. No one meeting him for the first time would ever assume that he was anything other than a suave and successful businessman. He hid the intimidating, formidable, tough-as-nails soldier that he'd been before he retired to start his own private investigations firm.

"Yes. He'll be in after lunch." Something in his father's question pinged on Niall's radar, so he asked, "Something up? Do you need him here now?"

He knew Jake would come in now if Alistair asked—he was their boss, after all—but Niall hoped whatever it was could wait until his partner got some much-needed shut-eye.

"Randy Richards showed up at his London townhouse this morning."

Niall stilled. "So that's where he ran off to from Rome," he murmured to himself.

"What's that?" Alistair lifted sharp eyes to his son's face.

Niall relayed what Jake had told him earlier. "Is he coming to buy or sell? Because he has managers running his business locally. What else could it be?" he wondered.

His father shook his head. "There've been no whispers from any of our sources about any increased trafficking movement from his organization this week. Intel continues to point to events unfolding abroad sometime in the next month, but nothing on British soil."

"So what are we thinking? Why is he back?"

"I've been looking into that," his father said. "We don't know a whole lot about this man aside from the stuff anyone looking for him can find. Only child, abusive father, absent mother, raised by a nanny. Run out of more than one prep school for criminal behavior..."

Niall interrupted. "Which translates into what specifically?"

"Sexual assault, suspected but never reported, producing and selling porn videos of those encounters, and one time," his father looked down at the paper he'd just picked up, "trying to organize a gang bang."

Niall recoiled in horror. "How old was he when that happened?"

"Seventeen." The disgust in Alistair's tone was plain to hear.

"How was he never arrested or charged?" Niall couldn't fathom it. "Who...?

His father answered the question he'd been about to ask next. "His father was a bigwig with a lot of influence. No doubt hush money changed hands. Where better to spend it than on the education of England's wealthiest little snots?" The sarcasm weighed down his father's words heavily. "Then, it's like he disappeared. No trace of him anywhere except at Cambridge, where he was the model student as far as anyone can tell. Didn't even seem to have a partner, male or female."

One of the things they had learned about Richards initially was that he was bisexual, which might explain why he did such a thriving business in both male and female prostitution and trafficking.

"Why are we looking at his personal life again? I thought we discounted any connection between his past—aside from the obvious—and his current crimes."

"My instinct tells me that this return is important. And since we've no new information about what's going to happen in the present, I thought it might be wise to go back to his past, to his history, to see if I could shake loose some reason for him to show up in the place he must know he's highly likely to be picked up and put away."

Niall sipped his tea and waited. His father hadn't wasted the time he'd spent in the SAS—the British equivalent of the American Delta Force—and his skills in analysis and detection were second to none. Their company wouldn't be what it had become without his expertise, and Niall had learned to trust his instincts.

"Something we didn't pay attention to before, but which may be significant now, is that Richards was married for a while."

Niall nodded. "I remember seeing that tidbit and wondering what woman in her right mind would marry a monster like that."

"Maybe when they married he was a better man?"

His father's sardonic tone made Niall laugh. Maybe Richards had been "better" when he was a young child, but if he was already into low-level prostitution and porn even as a teenager, the chances of him ever having been even "good" were slim to none.

"What does it say about the ex?"

His father picked up a different piece of paper and scanned it quickly. "Not a whole lot," he answered. "Married seven years, during which he apparently escalated his criminal activities."

"Was she a party to them?" Because if she was, maybe she was the reason he was back in town. "Maybe he's trying to mend fences so he can use her the way he's used every henchman we've caught. If the spotlight is on her, he can continue with business as usual while she gets to carry the bag for him."

Alistair nodded. "It's definitely something to look into, though the question of why he's suddenly decided to reconcile after seven years apart remains."

"Do we know her name?"

"The records say Antonia Renée Larson."

The phone on his desk interrupted him and Alistair picked it up, stepping away to speak to the person on the other line, but Niall didn't notice. His blood ran cold. Antonia Renée Larson... the name slammed into Niall's brain like a runaway train over a hapless car stuck on the tracks. Toni was their target's ex. What the actual hell was happening? Why hadn't she said anything to him? Why had she avoided talking about the man whenever the subject of her ex came up? Why had she never really explained what broke them apart? When was she going to come clean and tell him?

Granted, she didn't know he was after Richards, because he wasn't allowed to discuss the details of a case with people except on a need-to-know basis. Would she acknowledge the relationship when he asked? *If* he asked because how would he explain how he even knew who Richards was to her if he asked her about him?

This *had* to be a coincidence. His Toni couldn't be the same woman... He shut down the speculation. He would find out eventually, but for now, he had to focus on the conversation. He had a job to do, and his private life could not be allowed to distract him.

His father was speaking again. "The note says his ex is from the islands, which is where they married, though there's no marriage certificate in the file."

Something pricked at the back of Niall's brain, a niggling question, but he couldn't think about it just then. He wasn't even sure what had raised the hair on the back of his neck, but he'd come back to mull over the conversation later and maybe it would come to him.

"A sham marriage, maybe?" Would Toni be a party to something like that?

"If so, it was a sham for almost seven years."

"Wow!"

Niall couldn't imagine a scenario in which he'd be able to begin, let alone sustain, a fake relationship for seven years. And he couldn't imagine Toni involved in something shady like that. Especially not with all he already knew about her.

KT Bond | 45

"How old was she?" Richards was forty-six. If it wasn't Toni, perhaps the unknown woman was his age and desperate?

Once again, his father consulted the sheet of paper. "Birth certificate says she's thirty-six now, which means when they married she was merely twenty-two."

Dammit! That's how old Toni is. And the numbers add up... seven years married, seven divorced. That niggle in his brain grew sharper. Twenty-two... Richards' victims were all between the ages of fourteen and twenty-five. Fuck! Had he been planning on recruiting her? And if he had, what changed his mind? He took a deep breath to calm himself before speaking.

"That would have made him thirty-two when they got married." Niall shook his head. "I guess she likes older men."

Many young women did these days; many teenagers thought an older man meant greater experience and tenderness as well as the ability to support and care for them. He hated to think that Toni had been one of that group. He hated that thought with a passion.

"How can we find her?" He had a feeling he knew exactly where she lived, but he couldn't very well say that just then. He had to be sure. "I mean, if she knew then and divorced him or found out afterward what kind of man she'd been married to, maybe she moved away and changed her name. I can see a world where that's perfectly understandable." If wishes were horses, beggars would ride.

"Her last known address is where he still has a place in London." His father's voice broke into his thoughts again.

Niall sighed. "So, we don't have any record of where she lives, and I'm assuming whatever intel we have on her is spotty because no connection could be found between her and him professionally."

Alistair nodded. "Exactly. So we'll revisit the ex and see what we can find. Let's get on that immediately. Bring Jake up to speed when he comes in."

Niall nodded, silently running through every expletive he could think of as Alistair put the paper on his desk and clasped his hands in front of him. What was a good way to tell your best friend that the woman you were interested in was the ex-wife of a human trafficker, and that you were worried she'd once been a target of his organization?

"Speaking of exes..."

"Dad, don't." Niall sighed. He was definitely not ready to have this conversation at the moment, not when his mind was racing with awful possibilities.

Alistair grinned, unaware of his son's turmoil. Niall hadn't shared Toni's name with his family as yet. "What have I done, my boy?"

Niall shook his head, trying to dislodge the thoughts whirling in it. "It's what you're about to do that concerns me."

"I was just going to ask if your mother and I can expect you to bring anyone with you to dinner this Sunday."

"If I'm free..."

Niall paused, not knowing how to end the sentence. On the last two occasions on which he'd been free at the weekend to spend Sunday afternoon with his parents, he hadn't invited Toni to go along because he worried that it was too soon for her to be meeting them. He had told them he was seeing someone, and he understood their eagerness to finally meet her. But he and Toni had not seen each other a lot in the almost two months they'd been talking together. Much of their time was spent on video chat because he was away more than he was home.

Thoughts of Toni threatened to swamp him. Even if he wanted nothing more than to lose himself in fantasies about her, he wasn't about to do so in front of his father. And definitely not when there were so many questions about her possible relationship to his target.

"I'd have to ask her, see if she's available," he hedged.

He didn't need his father to know he was nixing the "meet the parents" moment until he was more certain of himself and of her. Thankfully, Alistair didn't question him further, merely accepting his response.

"You do that, son. And let your mother know ASAP. You know how she gets."

Niall nodded. He did know and he would do everything he could to avoid his mother having even one anxious moment. But as he walked back to his own office, he let his mind wander to thoughts of Toni Larson, the woman he had met less than eight weeks earlier and who had captured his imagination. They'd been mutually attracted from the first time they laid eyes on each other, and the dates and chats they'd enjoyed since then were cementing something warm and sweet and passionate between them.

Their very first date, when he had taken her to Jake's party in their friend's backyard, had been a revelation for him. Niall couldn't speak for Toni, but *his* emotions had played havoc with his concentration and sociability all afternoon, and more than once Jake had had to pull his proverbial coattails to get him back in the game. Warmth flooded his chest at the memories as he returned to his own office to tackle paperwork that never seemed to go away.

He'd have to call her later, see what she thought of the idea. If he could couch it in less forbidding terms than "meeting the parents," she might not object. He knew he couldn't omit that bit of information or she'd balk, and he wasn't prepared to be told no, not after all they'd already done to be where they were with each other. And he'd be damned if this Richards guy was going to fuck things up.

He pulled up the last file he'd been working on, reading to see where he'd left off and trying to focus on work, but Toni was firmly lodged in his head, so he let her have free rein. He'd get back to business when Jake came in.

"Mac?"

He looked up, noticing Jake standing in the doorway of his office. His friend's low voice rattled him out of the momentary stupor he'd fallen into.

"Yeah? What's up?"

"That's my question, dude. You look like you've just seen a ghost."

Niall shook himself slightly, trying to dislodge the deep fear that sank into his bones. Would Toni keep something like this from him? Did she even know what her ex was into?

"Mac! What's wrong, man?"

Jake's tone was urgent now as he sat across from him, and Niall responded to it with a huff.

"Nothing."

He knew his best friend wasn't going to believe him, but he wasn't ready to talk about this with anyone just yet. He needed a moment—more, really—to figure out what all the emotions that were battling in his chest meant, to figure out how he would address the news with Toni, to decide whether or not he had to recuse himself from the case. While he was thinking, he slid the paper with the information that had stopped him cold across the desk to Jake, who took it and read it. He whistled low when he was done.

"Shit! Is this... is Richards's ex your woman?"

Niall swallowed and nodded, suddenly unable to speak.

"Damn! I'm guessing you're just finding out and now you're second guessing yourself and her, yeah?"

One more nod. Niall's mouth was dry, his chest tight, his lungs screaming for air.

"Shouldn't you talk to her before you make assumptions and judgments?"

He should, shouldn't he? Why hadn't he thought of that? He wished the suggestion made him feel better.

CHAPTER 5

The next week was torture as Niall forced himself to focus on work and not the woman he knew was waiting for him to call. One phone conversation was all he'd managed before things got busier than anticipated. And truth be told, he had avoided calling her because he still had no idea how to ask her about her ex. He had only managed to send a quick apology text message, and when Toni didn't respond, fear and anger fought for pride of place in his heart.

What was she thinking? He'd told her what he did for a living, and she knew he had to go away sometimes. Did she think he was blowing her off? Surely she had to know that was as far from the case as it could be? Hadn't his kisses told her that he was as caught in her web as surely as a wild animal in a trap? The thought of being at her mercy didn't exactly sit well with him, although he knew she didn't see him as prey... at least he didn't think she did.

This business with Randy Richards wasn't helping, either. Was she the phantom wife? How was he going to raise the question with her without compromising his job? Should he even be seeing her if she was a material witness? Damn! Second guessing himself was for the birds. It didn't work in his job, and it wasn't helping him now in the love life he was trying to jumpstart. As soon as he got back, he called her, but he had to leave a message because she didn't pick up. What could she be doing that she couldn't answer a simple phone call?

His message—"I'm back. Call me when you can"—was terse, but he couldn't think what else to say without sounding like a possessive jerk. Even if he thought it was okay to be possessive, they didn't have that kind of relationship yet. And if he didn't play his cards right, he was sure that they never would. Toni didn't strike him as the type to suffer fools gladly.

She didn't return his call for another three days. Niall fumed and snapped, a bear with a sore head, assuming the worst like a green boy. Maybe she was back in contact with his target. After all, what did he really know about her? He couldn't credit it, though. That was just not the vibe she gave him.

When she finally responded and left a message—because he was in a meeting and couldn't answer her—she sounded like death warmed over when he called back. He rushed over to her place with soup and a sandwich. He had never had this reaction to any other woman before. The need to care for her overwhelmed him. She was hot to the touch and shivering when she opened the door to him, and he placed the bag with the food on the little table by her front door, picking her up and taking her back to her bedroom.

She was sweaty and a little gross, but he didn't care. He found her bathroom and wet a washcloth, coming back to sponge off her face and neck. He smoothed her hair away from her face and leaned in.

"What did you take for the fever?"

"Nothing. I just had a cup of ginger tea and came to bed."

He went back into her bathroom and found the over-the-counter pills for fever and pain. He took two and went to the kitchen to get water. On the way there, he remembered the food he'd brought, so he went to get that, too. Reheating a cup of the soup, he took everything back into the bedroom with him.

Toni was dozing, her body curved in the fetal position. He set everything down on her side table and sat next to her. When she stirred, he pulled her up and wrapped his arm around her.

"You need to take these pills and drink a little of the soup before you go back to sleep, Toni."

"I'm tired." She rubbed her eyes like a child.

"I know, love, but I'll help you, okay?"

He managed to get her to swallow the pills, but she had only had a few spoonfuls of the soup before she was turning her head away. He gave up trying to feed her and set her back against the pillows. Immediately, she turned and curled over on herself. He wished he could be the big spoon and wrap her up with his body, but he didn't need to get whatever she had come down with. And anyway, he didn't think she'd appreciate him inviting himself to share her bed, no matter how innocuous the reason.

The next time she woke up, she was sweating again, but she seemed to be somewhat more alert. He knew she'd feel a whole lot better after she'd had a bath, so while she finished the soup he had reheated once again, he set a bath for her.

"Which of these bath salts do you want me to add to the water?" he asked her, walking back into the bedroom with the three bottles he'd found. He had no idea about such things.

"Jasmine," she told him with a weak smile.

When the bath was full enough, he led her into the bathroom.

"Can you manage on your own?"

She looked much steadier on her feet, and though he wanted nothing more than to strip her of every piece of clothing she was wearing, this wasn't how he'd envisioned getting to that goal. He wanted her healthy when he indulged that fantasy. Turning away when she nodded, he made sure to let her know he wouldn't be far if she needed him.

"Call me if you need me."

He found pajamas and laid them out on her bed but resisted the urge to search for underwear. He'd have to let her find those on her own if he was going to avoid intruding into her private space any more than he had already done. He would see if she'd come out to eat so he could remake her bed before she went back into it. Nothing felt worse than a clean body on sweaty sheets.

He made a fresh grilled cheese sandwich for her, reheated the rest of the soup, and was setting everything out on the table when she walked in. She looked a lot better, though her eyes were still tired, and she was still shivering.

"Here. Come sit."

He pulled the chair out for her, and once she was comfortably settled, he sat across from her with the store-bought sandwich for him and a cup of coffee.

"Eat up. When was the last time you had a meal?"

Pausing with the spoon halfway to her mouth, she thought for a second before answering. "Yesterday. I had some leftover spaghetti for dinner."

"Does your throat hurt?" he asked when she winced as she sipped the soup.

"A bit, yes. But the soup is helping. Don't think I can handle that, though," she continued, pointing at the sandwich.

"One thing at a time," he admonished her gently. "Finish your soup and we'll figure out the rest later."

She did as she was bid, and though she protested at first when he asked where she kept her bed linens, he was adamant.

"You don't need to be making beds right now. You just need sustenance and sleep."

Once the bed was made, he helped her back into it and before she dozed off again, he said, "I'm going to go, but I'll be back in the morning. If you need me before then, call me."

"I'll be fine, Niall," she began but he interrupted her.

"Call me. Promise." He waited until she sighed and nodded before continuing. "I'll come back early in the morning. Do you have a spare set of keys? I can let myself in, and I'll return them when I come in the morning."

He saw her hesitation and could imagine some of the things going through her head. What if he made a copy of them? He could come back while she was out and empty her apartment. Or he could show up unannounced and take advantage of her. Anything was possible, and she was right to be cautious. He wouldn't insist if she refused his request, even if he wanted to. He didn't plan to give her any reason to mistrust him.

"How early are you planning to come by?" she asked.

"Seven. I'll be on my way to work, but I just need to make sure you're okay for the day."

"Niall, you really don't need to ..."

"You don't get to tell me what I need to do and what I don't," he told her. "I know what I need, and it is to make sure you're set for the day." He looked at her sternly. "So, if you won't give me the spare keys, you'll need to answer the door at seven when I get here."

She nodded after another long moment of thought. "Okay."

Niall thought she was agreeing to open the door for him when he got there, so her next words surprised him.

"The keys are inside the hall closet on a hook just inside the door." She smiled at him. "If anything happens to me, the security cameras will see who was the last person here, and Karen will come hunt you down. So really, I know I'll be completely safe with you."

Niall laughed. "Thanks for the vote of confidence. Sleep sweet, love."

He didn't bother to remind her that with the kind of job he did, getting into her apartment wouldn't be too difficult even without a key. That knowledge wouldn't serve his cause well. He dropped a quick kiss on her forehead, went to check the refrigerator so he would know if he needed to bring her anything for breakfast, and slipped out of the flat.

She was still asleep when he returned the next morning. He dropped his windbreaker over the back of the couch and went to make breakfast. He brewed tea and sliced bread for toast and then went to see if she was awake. He found her just getting out of bed.

"Hey, good morning. Need help?" He waited by the door for her to answer.

"No, I'm okay. Thank you."

She scurried away and he grinned, assuming she needed to relieve her bladder. He didn't need to hear that, so he went back to the kitchen and finished breakfast. She could probably handle an omelet, and he'd make himself some toast to go with his.

"Good morning." Her voice behind him made him turn to look at her. "You know you don't need to feed me, right?" she asked. She sounded a little raspy, but she looked better than she had when he'd left the night before.

"I know. But since I haven't eaten yet, I thought I'd kill two birds with one stone."

He turned back to the eggs he'd been whipping and poured some of it for the first omelet into the skillet. She walked over to the cupboard and pulled out cups and saucers and plates. As she was setting the table for two, he finished the omelets and set the bread to toast.

"Can you handle a slice of toast with this?" he asked, turning to set the omelets on the table.

"I'll have my bread soft, please. With butter."

They didn't speak again until she had finished her omelet and half of the slice of bread and butter. Niall polished off the other half, making her chuckle. When he got up to clear away the dishes, she spoke firmly.

"Niall, I can tidy up. Shouldn't you be on your way?"

Was she trying to get rid of him? Had he overstepped somewhere? Was she expecting company? Uncertainty gripped him, and he hated how this new knowledge that he had was making him think twice about everything she said. He chose to give in, nodded, and walked back into the living room to get his windbreaker, shrugging into it before turning to find her watching him. He smiled at her and held out her key.

"Here you go. Thanks for letting me use it."

"Thanks for returning it," she answered. "And for looking after me. I appreciate it."

"I'll come by with dinner later, so you won't have to bother with cooking today, okay? Just get some rest."

"Don't you have weekends off?" she asked him as he strode to the door. "It's Saturday."

"It is, but I need to finish some paperwork. So, dinner later. Any special requests?"

"Nothing too spicy. My throat is still a bit sore. Something easy, like pasta?"

"Pasta it is. Get some rest, Toni." He resisted the urge to lean in for a kiss, even one on the cheek. Last night, she'd been a bit out of it when he'd kissed her forehead, but she was alert today, and he suddenly felt unsure of how she would respond. "Later."

He slipped out the door before she could answer, hoping she didn't take offense at his hasty retreat. Thinking about how upset he'd been when Toni hadn't returned his call, he admitted that he'd been acting like an immature teenager. Was this what being attracted to her was doing to him? What did it mean that he couldn't control his emotions around her? And when would he get a chance to broach the subject of her ex?

Resolving never to make a snap judgment about her silences in the future, he spent the rest of the day doggedly completing the backlog of paperwork on his desk. He managed to get it all done and was pleased he hadn't needed to leave any for his assistant to finish on Monday. As he was completing the last of it, he made a takeaway order to pick up on his way to Toni's flat.

Toni had already set the table for dinner when Niall got there later that evening, so once they'd helped themselves, they talked about their expectations regarding messages going forward. The conversation started awkwardly.

"We need to talk," he said, "but let's eat first." He sounded reluctant to begin.

She chuckled. "We can't talk and eat? Are you dumping me but making sure to fatten me up for the kill first?" she asked, trying to lighten the mood.

She could see that he wasn't amused. "Do I seem like the kind of man to feed you before I dump you?"

She gave him a long, assessing stare, and she watched as the pulse in his throat kicked up. Was he feeling as completely unnerved as she was? She couldn't remember ever starting a conversation with any man that had her feeling so unsettled. She chose to answer him seriously.

"Actually, not to be a jerk, but yes. It's precisely because you are the kind of man you are that you'd make sure I was fed and watered before kicking me to the curb." He pinned her with a chastening glare, but she finished the thought. "But I guess you don't strike me as the kind of man who would bring me dinner to begin with if you were actually going to say goodbye."

He seemed somewhat mollified as he replied, "Unless you have some deeply-buried secret that you know would make us being together impossible, then this is not an in-person version of a Dear Jane letter."

She hoped he didn't notice the way she flinched. She knew she was keeping a secret from him, but it was only so she could protect him. She could see him trying to read her expression, but she looked down at the fork as she swirled pasta around on it, only raising it to her lips when she was sure that her eyes were clear and her expression free from anything that could be called guilt.

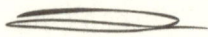

Niall, for his part, hoped that it had been his imagination when he'd thought she flinched at his question. He was so far gone over her, even after such a short time, that he knew the fallout if they ended things would likely break him wide open. That was not a comfortable thought.

Did he really want to be this vulnerable with a woman he'd only known a month? And what could he do to pull back, to rein in his wild emotions where she was concerned? How could he take back control of the heart he hadn't even realized until this moment that he'd been about to hand over to her? This conversation could definitely not be happening at a better time than now.

"So, what's so important you had to preface it with those words of doom-not-doom?" Toni brought the conversation back around to his opening remark.

He decided to be direct. Better that than have her trying to parse out his meaning.

"I hate it when you don't answer my texts..." He paused, trying to find a good way to say what came next. "...quickly." He hurried on before she could respond. "I know that I've been late answering yours as well, but honestly, I hate waiting."

She gazed at him unblinkingly before she answered. "Patience is a virtue, so they say, but I'm with you on that." She paused to stare him down again before adding, "I guess it's important to clear the air so we can be more comfortable going forward."

"So, just to be clear, if I don't answer your call or text right away, it's because I'm working or I'm somewhere that I can't answer, okay?" He ignored the little voice in his head pointing out that he'd just basically set a standard that he couldn't ignore if he wanted to keep seeing her.

"Okay. And the same goes for me."

One problem addressed. Niall prayed that every other potential difficulty—a.k.a. talking about her ex, the human trafficker—would be as easily addressed going forward. Common sense said he was dreaming. Hope cheered in encouragement. They finished dinner amicably, did the dishes together, and then he sat with her to watch *Call the Midwife* as he had promised her he would do. They cuddled together on her sofa, her warm body heating his own, making him wish for things he probably couldn't have.

Niall found himself torn between a rising desire to disturb her restfulness with ravenous kisses and a real interest in the happenings on the screen. He forced himself to pay attention to the show, holding his body stiffly though he didn't pull his arm away from her.

As the credits rolled, he tried to dispel the haze of lust that had gathered around him and asked, "Is it always this intense?"

Toni nodded. "Every week we get an intimate look into the hearts of the sisters, the nurses, and the people they care for. I love it!"

"I really like how the show seems to take on hard problems," he said. "That family was so torn up because the son felt his parents wouldn't love him anymore because he's gay. I felt really bad for his parents, as well. When he checked himself into that clinic..."

Toni took his hand, as if she realized that he couldn't finish the sentence. He didn't watch much television—he didn't have the time, to be honest—and when he did watch, it was mostly police procedurals, thrillers, or documentaries. So, he was pleasantly surprised that such good shows were on.

"I'm glad you liked it," she said simply.

Niall knew it was time to leave, but he couldn't make himself move. He was too comfortable and the emotions rolling around inside him left him feeling exposed and raw. He closed his eyes briefly, then inhaled and opened them, pulling gently away from her to stand.

"I'd better be off. Sunday dinner at my parents' place. Would you like to come?"

What the hell, Niall? That had not been anywhere close to what he meant to say, but the invitation was out now and he couldn't take it back. He still didn't think they were even ready for her to meet the parents. Apparently, though, despite what his brain said about his readiness, his heart was on board with it.

Doing his best not to panic, he waited for her answer, and barely restrained the sigh of relief when she said, "Not this time. I need one more day of full rest so I'll be at a hundred percent on Monday."

She stood with him and followed him to the door. "Thanks for dinner and for staying after to watch TV with me, Niall. This was a really sweet date."

He inclined his head with a smile. He liked that she thought of it as a date. "My pleasure. Let me know if there's anything else I can do for you between now and then, okay?"

She eyed him speculatively and he wondered what she was thinking. He didn't have long to wait.

"Well, you can start by giving me a kiss good-night. That is how dates end, isn't it?"

All thoughts of ex-husbands and uncomfortable revelations fled as Niall pulled her to him with a groan and laid his lips on hers, letting out all the pent-up desire of the evening, turning to push her up against the wall so he could ravish her without risking her falling. She was still not completely well, after all, and he could be a gentleman when he needed to be. But he didn't hold back on the kiss, uncaring that he could, in fact, get whatever bug she had.

"Mmm," she moaned against his mouth when he let her up for air.

"If you don't let me go, I may not leave, Toni," he warned her, nipping her lips as he did so.

When she groaned and widened her stance against the wall, he growled and plunged back in for another kiss, slotting his hips between her spread thighs and rolling up against her hungry warmth. She hissed and pushed back against him.

He tore his lips from hers. "Be sure, love," he whispered raggedly. "Be really sure."

CHAPTER 6

T oni felt sure. She'd never felt more certain of anything than she was that she wanted to lie with Niall in her bed and let him take her apart so he could put her back together again. She needed it. After her divorce, when she'd been a walking shadow of herself, she had shied away from men completely, refusing even to go out for coffee with them. Outside of the requirements of her job, she'd become a hermit, until she had decided to indulge without committing.

"I'm really sure, Niall. I want..." she paused, gazing steadfastly into his eyes so he could see how serious she was, "I need you now."

She realized, even as he cupped her cheeks in his warm hands and kissed her tenderly, that she did need him. She was a strong woman, and she knew, especially post-Randy, that she didn't need anyone, male or female, to make her happy or help her feel complete. But she was also adult enough to know that she could find greater support, satisfaction, and love, if she opened herself to someone trustworthy who saw and cherished her strength, who valued her independence, and who would care about and for her unselfishly.

"I'm here for anything you need, any time, love."

Niall's words were a clear promise that she knew instinctively he'd keep no matter what happened between them. He was so much more than the hookups she had allowed herself to have when her electric lover wore out its welcome or was just not enough to satisfy her need for human touch. When he leaned in to capture her lips again, she let herself forget everything else so that she could focus on what he was doing to her with his hands and his lips, and before she was even sure her body was ready, he was stroking inside her in slow, steady thrusts. His arms caged her in, and tears sprang to her eyes when she recognized how much she had missed being held like this.

Was this why she was letting him in before she was sure she was ready for this level of intimacy? She was sure she wanted him. She was sure he wanted her. As far as those two things went, her answer had been true. But was she as sure she was ready to be so open and vulnerable with a man whom she was only now getting to know better?

Toni kept her eyes closed so Niall wouldn't see how deeply moved she was or that she was suddenly wavering, and she didn't want him to think he was hurting her in any way. She worked herself on his invading rod, needing to forget her sudden uncertainty and embrace her body's needs, answering his plunges into her heated depths with her own upward thrusts, holding onto him so that his withdrawals stroked every place he touched, raising the lust between them. She squeezed him with every inward push, loving the way he groaned and grunted in response.

"You're gonna make me come, Toni," he whispered against her lips.

"Wasn't that the plan?" she panted in response, lifting her legs and wrapping them around his waist, all the while giving him back stroke for stroke.

"Not before you do, love." He paused, his cock deep inside her, and demanded, "Look at me." When she opened her eyes, happy that no tears escaped, he added, "I need to take care of you."

It was as if he'd heard her thoughts a moment ago and was telling her what she wanted to hear. Fresh tears welled up and Niall swiped away the ones that escaped her control, leaning in to kiss her eyes closed again.

"I hope it's okay that I want to take care of you," he continued. "I know you can take care of yourself, but will you let me help you, at least?"

This was the strangest conversation to be having with a man balls deep inside her, but it felt like the one they needed to have just then. He needed reassurance that she wouldn't reject his care. How sweet was that!

"Yes." She leaned up and bit his lip. "Now move, please?"

Niall's growl echoed around them as he gave her what she wanted, taking her over and over, kissing her everywhere his mouth could reach. He stroked into her deep and hard, going faster and faster until she was mindless with lust and aching with the need to climax.

"Niall!" She called out to him, desperate for the orgasm his body promised her.

"Come for me, love," he said against her lips, canting his hips and hitting her g-spot over and over with each thrust.

Toni held back the scream of fulfillment that wanted to rip itself from her, the restrained sound making her throat ache.

"No! Let me hear you, baby! Scream for me."

"Ahhhhhh!" Toni obeyed, holding on to him while he rocked her world.

Niall's own shout of completion sent new shivers of awareness racing through her as she came down from the high of the first orgasm that she'd had with a man that had meant more than just a physical release since well before her divorce. Thoughts of her last almost-relationship with Eric were like a bucket of cold water over her. He had been the first and only man she'd been on more than one date with since her divorce, and his untimely death had ended her efforts to start anything serious again. Nothing with Eric had been this good, though, and it was freaking her out.

Niall must have felt her withdrawal because he pulled slowly out of her, holding on to her so she didn't collapse to the floor. Damn... she'd just let a man she barely knew fuck her up against a wall, quick and dirty, like a trick and his two-bit hooker. The raw thought struck her like a whip across her chest, and she gasped as though she had felt the sting of it.

"Are you alright, Toni?"

Niall's concern bled through his words, and she forced herself to look up into his eyes and answer.

"I'm fine." She struggled to find something to say that would erase the harsh thought that she'd just let escape. "That was ... good. Really good. I'm just a bit overwhelmed is all. It's been a while."

She could see the suspicion in his gaze, and she knew he had every right not to believe her, but she prayed he'd accept her half-truths anyway.

"Come on. Let's get cleaned up."

He stepped away from her and took her hand. His silence was unnerving, but Toni had nothing to offer to make it less uncomfortable for herself, so she followed him into the shower, let him wash her and then stepped out again and dried off, pulling a robe over her body and sitting on the edge of the bed to wait for him. She felt exposed, somehow, agitated and unsettled by the emotions that rolled around inside her.

"Ready to talk?"

Niall's voice in front of her dragged her eyes open. He was fully dressed again, and his eyes held both understanding and disappointment. She nodded, not bothering to question how he knew she needed to talk. He knew for sure that he was the one needing to talk. Either way, she rose and walked with him into the living room, aware that she was naked under the robe except for a very sensible pair of white panties. Somehow, she knew they wouldn't be revisiting the passion that had overwhelmed them an hour ago.

She hurried to begin, not wanting him to start the conversation with words she wasn't ready to hear.

"Please don't think poorly of me, Niall, but I think maybe we've gotten a bit ahead of ourselves."

He studied her for a moment before replying. "How so?"

She had a feeling he knew what she meant, but for whatever reason, he wanted her to say it openly. It wouldn't make a difference whether she articulated her feelings plainly or not... emotionally, she hadn't been ready for sex with him. She had let her hormones get the better of her, and now she had made things awkward and potentially killed whatever had begun to grow between them.

"I should have let you leave earlier when you wanted to. What we just did together wasn't part of the plan, and I'm afraid it's messed things up." She looked away from him, down to her hands, fingers twisting in her lap. "I'm really not that woman, Niall. I don't lead men on."

"So, what are you saying, Toni?"

His voice had no inflection. Was he angry? Toni took a deep breath and plunged on. However he chose to respond to her next words, she still had to say them.

"I don't think we should ... do that again. Not until we really know each other well enough to know it's the best thing to do. It was too soon, at least for me. The last thing I want to do is hurt you, and I definitely don't want to set myself up for any more pain than I've already lived through, you know? So, can we just be friends for now? Please?"

More than anything, she needed Niall to understand and agree. She didn't want to lose him, especially not as a friend. Now the ball was in his court.

Niall inhaled sharply. "So, just to be clear, we won't make love again until you're sure that you're ready to go all the way, yes?" When she nodded, speechless with embarrassment, he went on. "How will you know when you're sure next time? Because you said you were when I asked before."

Toni flinched at the hard note in his voice when he said that. He was right. He had wanted to be sure of his own position when he'd asked, and she had assured him that she was certain, thus giving him the consent he needed. If he was angry now, that was all on her. There was no way she could escape the blame for what had happened.

"How will *I* know?" he continued. Another great question for which she had no ready answer. "And what are we allowed to do together that won't send you scuttling away?"

Although his tone had gone back to being neutral, Toni was almost certain that Niall was seething with pent-up emotions. Whether anger, frustration, disappointment or impatience, or a combination of all of them, she didn't know, but she could feel the energy of his restraint beating against her.

She wanted to reassure him that she wasn't pulling away from him, that she was just slowing things down until she felt more stable emotionally, but she didn't think anything else she had to say would improve the situation at that point.

So instead, she tried to find sensible, non-hurtful answers to his perfectly valid questions.

"Maybe we can take it in stages? You know, instead of jumping into the sack immediately, we can ramp up the experiences."

His eyes lit up with some emotion she was too distraught to read. "You mean, we should just extend foreplay until you say when?"

That made sense, she supposed, even if it sounded cold and cruel, but she agreed. What else was she to do? His next words left her feeling even more twisted up inside again.

"I'm a red-blooded man, Toni. You're asking me to endure some degree of sexual frustration for an indeterminate amount of time while you figure out what you're really ready for with me. Does that about sum it up? What else can I look forward to while I wait for you to be ready?"

Ouch! Yeah... he was definitely upset. Based on his questions, though, at least he didn't seem to be about to bail on her. Toni's head hurt and her eyes burned with unshed tears of frustration for the mess she had made. And added to all that was a small spurt of irritation with him that he seemed to think he was the only one who would suffer. She went with that feeling... better to sound off about that than allow her remorse to get the better of her.

"You're not the only one who'll be frustrated, you know. We're in this together." She had wanted to sound annoyed, but it came out resigned instead. Not what she was trying to convey.

He reached for her hand then, sighing heavily as if her words had broken down a wall he'd been building to keep her out.

"Thank you for saying that. I'm glad I'm not alone. I just need to be certain that you mean it."

"I do mean it. I'd like to give us a real chance, but I want to be a hundred percent on board and not just be ruled by desire. I'm a big girl... I can handle it."

He stood up then and reached for her hand. "Come see me out?"

This time, he kept the kiss goodnight to her cheeks. "Remember what I said, Toni." He tipped her chin up so he could look her in the eye as he repeated his promise. "I'm here for anything you need, any time. Okay?"

She smiled, feeling better about how things were ending this time. "Okay. Thank you."

He touched his lips to hers then before speaking again. "Get some sleep. I'll call you as often as I can. Goodnight, love."

CHAPTER 7

W hen the phone rang two days later as Toni was finishing her meal prep for dinner, she hurried to answer it. She had been in a tizzy ever since Niall had left her house and she'd needed someone to talk to. All she'd told Karen in the hurried voice message she'd left her was that she needed to talk. She knew her friend would call back when she could.

"Hello."

She stuck the phone between her shoulder and her ear as she finished making the salad and covered it before sticking it into the fridge. The meat was simmering in marinara sauce and the pasta needed another four minutes or so.

"Toni? It's me. What's going on?" Karen's concern was evident in her voice.

She didn't know where to begin. "It's about Niall and me." That at least was accurate. "I... we..."

"Wow! I've never known you to be made speechless by a man before. And it's been more than a month, and you're still with him, so I guess this could become serious, huh?"

"Yes, it could. But I think I messed up the last time we were together, and I'm worried that it'll be harder for him to trust me now."

"What did you do?"

Karen's very reasonable question made Toni's head hurt. "I slept with him."

A small silence followed before Karen answered her. "Okay." She dragged out the word, clearly confused. "And that's messing up how exactly?"

Toni sighed. Karen knew she'd been fairly free with her favors before, and though she had never interfered or offered unsolicited advice, Toni knew her friend worried about her hookups. She could well understand Karen's confusion since sleeping with a man had never been an issue before.

"I told him it was a mistake and that I needed to slow things down."

"Ouch! Oh dear!" Sympathy colored Karen's voice as she continued. "I take it that didn't go over well? He doesn't strike me as the kind of man to take rejection well, from the little I know of him."

"He was upset, yes. But he agreed to go slower."

"So what's the problem, if he agreed?"

"Would you trust someone who's done that to you to be real with you afterward? Wouldn't you question everything he says going forward? Wouldn't he have to prove himself?" She felt a kind of panic rising inside her. "What the hell can I do to prove to him that I'm not that woman who leads men on and then drops them when I lose interest? That I'm not a heartbreaker?"

She moved the phone from her ear, putting it on speaker and propping it on the stand she had in the kitchen for times when she needed to talk and work. She pulled the pasta from the stove, draining it before adding it to the meat sauce and coating it completely. A minute or two more and it would be ready.

"I don't think I'm the one you should be asking that question, Toni. It sounds to me like Niall is important to you, so you should ask him what you need to do to make him trust you completely. And I think you shouldn't wait to ask, either. The longer you put off the hard conversation, the more difficult it will be to have it. I speak from experience."

Toni knew Karen's story of how she had kept her true feelings from the man she'd been last engaged to and how his death had caused her both relief and guilt.

"I know. I just don't want to mess things up any more than they already are, you know?"

"Look, no matter what happens, things can't be better between you if you don't talk to him. You know what they say about the top reason relationships fall apart, right? You're the counselor."

This was why she needed to talk to her friend. Karen was sensible, level-headed, and at a point in her life where she was only interested in honest communication between two consenting adults. Toni knew she was right... she had to talk to Niall, find out what he was feeling, what he needed from her going forward.

"Yes, I am," she agreed, "and you're right. I'll talk to him the next time I see him in person."

She didn't think that that was a conversation she should have over the phone while he was away on business. She'd just have to deal with her anxiety until she saw him again.

"I'll invite him over for dinner and we'll talk then. Wish me luck."

"Good luck," Karen said obediently, and they both chuckled.

"So, anything new on the Dutch front?" Toni asked next. She was curious about how her friend's love life was going.

"Nothing as exciting as your story," Karen answered with a laugh. "We've just been emailing. He's a really smart man."

"And you like them nerdy like you, I know," Toni teased.

"I like a man with a big brain," Karen answered, making Toni laugh.

"A big brain, huh? That's different!"

"Hush up, hussy!" Karen said, but she was laughing, too.

Toni felt a lot better, though everything Karen had suggested was what she had known she must do. She'd just needed it confirmed by someone who wasn't involved, someone she could trust who wasn't her mother. This was not something she could share with her mother, whom she knew would always have her back, no matter what.

"Well, thanks for calling me back, Karen. I hope things work out for you and your Dutchman, too. I'll let you know what happens with Niall."

"Thanks. I'm sure everything will work out. You're both smart people. You'll know if it's worth pursuing more with each other."

"From your mouth to God's ears," Toni said.

"Based on the little I know of him, I'd say Niall doesn't suffer fools gladly. So if he's still around, he'll appreciate your effort to be real with him," Karen told her confidently.

Toni felt curiously relieved by her friend's assessment. Karen was usually right about people. "Thanks, love. Please give my best to George and Elaine."

"Will do."

She was on tenterhooks for the next couple of days until Niall called as she was getting ready for bed. It had been a long day and she'd been more than ready to fall into the soft sheets and let go. She answered the phone before settling her back against the pillows mounded up at the headboard.

"Hey, Toni. Sorry I'm calling so late, but I didn't want another day to pass without checking in and I'm going back out in about an hour. How have you been?"

The sound of his voice made something warm and sweet well in her chest. She loved how just hearing him seemed to settle her spirit.

"I'm tired. Today was extra long and very busy. But I'm about ready to go to bed now."

"I should be home in a couple of days. Will you be rested enough to go out with me?"

"I'll do my best. But how about you come by for dinner when you get home first?"

Toni almost added "We need to talk," but wisely kept silent. The last thing Niall needed while he was on the job was to be distracted by worrying about what bad news she had to give him.

"I'll call you when I land. Then you can tell me what you need me to do."

"Sounds good."

"See you soon, love. Get some sleep now."

"Goodnight, Niall. Be safe."

"Always, love."

Toni missed him fiercely. She didn't know when it happened, but she was glad she hadn't spoken the words that were cold comfort to her when she hung up. Did he miss her? He hadn't said anything to make her think he had, and she knew she couldn't expect that from him, particularly after the last time. She fell asleep to thoughts of what she could make to tempt him when he arrived.

Two more days of hard work, including talking a client out of running and putting herself and her unborn child in harm's way, and she was ready for the weekend. Niall hadn't called and she was stressing over what to make for him. Finally, because she needed something to do to stop herself from thinking the worst, she decided she'd make lasagna and do some fried chicken wings with fried potato wedges, in case he didn't fancy Italian food. She fell asleep on the couch waiting for his call, shuddering awake when her cell phone vibrated on her belly. She answered, still groggy.

"Hello?"

"Toni, it's Niall. Sorry I'm calling so late."

Toni passed a hand over her face and sat up. "What time is it?"

"Half one in the morning. I'm just leaving the airport. How soon do you want me there later?"

She registered the fact that he sounded tired and managed to stop herself from saying, "You can come now," because she was wide awake now and there'd be no excuse for that ill-timed invitation.

"When you wake up, give me a call," she said instead.

"Sounds good. Talk soon, love."

Why had she thought it wouldn't be the most awkward reunion? As Niall walked into her flat later, Toni ran her damp palms over the jeans she was wearing and forced herself not to give any other signs of anxiety. After all, Niall was an investigator, and he would probably be able to read her body language.

He turned and watched her approach him where he had stopped in the middle of the living room. The flowers he was holding were a riotous assortment of colors.

"Are those for me?" *Stupid! Of course they're for you, idiot! Way to hide how nervous you are.*

A small smile curved Niall's lips, but he only said, "Yes" and handed them to her. She took them, feeling incredibly foolish, and walked into the kitchen to get a vase for them. Niall followed her, leaning against the kitchen island and watching her as she filled the blue glass vase with water, added the plant food, and arranged the flowers in it.

"I'll just go put these on the coffee table."

She hurried away like a petty criminal from a crime scene. When she returned to the kitchen, Niall reached for her as she made to step past him.

"Okay, you need to tell me what's going on. Why are you so on edge?"

He held her by her elbows, stopping her from moving away from him. Toni sighed inwardly. Guess it was time for the talk.

"Nothing is going on, exactly," she began. "I just... we need to talk. That's all."

He let her go then and went to sit on one of the bar stools at the island. She looked over to find him watching her, his gaze hooded. She stayed where she had stopped by the table, not liking that she couldn't read his expression, though she was fairly certain he was preparing himself to hear bad news.

"Shoot."

He leaned back against the countertop, his arms crossed over his chest, waiting for her to begin. She took a deep breath, wishing she didn't feel like a naughty child summoned to explain her misbehavior to the headmaster.

"I've been very ... worried about what happened between us," she began. "I know I seem to be sending mixed messages, and I'm afraid that you may still have the impression that I'm one of those people who uses other people and then discards them when she loses interest. I just want to reassure you that I'm not like that at all."

She paused, feeling fresh anxiety that he would remain suspicious of her motives. Words were never enough in a situation like this. The thought of losing what they had begun to establish between them made her breathless with fear.

"I know you'll need more than my word because we still don't know each other well enough and we haven't spent a lot of time together. So, I just want to know how I can prove myself to you."

Niall held her gaze for a long moment before speaking. She felt exposed but she bore his scrutiny as calmly as she could. She wouldn't hide from him, not now when it was so important to build trust between them.

"Maybe if you explain to me why you were waffling about before, I can understand you better. Trust is earned, but sometimes it can be given a helping hand. With all the relevant facts at my disposal, I'll be in a better position to decide."

"I am very attracted to you, Niall," she began, choosing her words carefully. "And when you asked me if I was sure I wanted to be with you, I said I was because it was true. I was overwhelmed with the need to be touched, but even more, I wanted you to be the one touching me, holding me, making me feel loved."

She looked up quickly, hastening to reassure him. "Not that I'm saying you love me or anything, but..."

"I know what you mean, Toni." Niall's voice was calm. "Go on."

"I know that love and sex aren't the same thing. I know they can exist independently of each other. And like I said that night, I didn't want it just to be a hookup. I wanted sex with you to mean something more. But I didn't let that happen that night, and I knew if I let it go, I would never address it and things would get awkward between us. But please know I do want all the things with you that you think I do."

"Based on what you told me when we first met, you haven't been celibate since your divorce. So, what changed?"

Fair question, but she didn't like how he sounded like a detective grilling a suspect. How should she answer him? It wasn't a question she had even thought of until he asked it.

"I'm not sure," she told him honestly. "I just feel that you are someone I can build something with, and I don't want to confuse the issue with sex."

"For the record, I wasn't confused when I was with you that time," he said, his eyes holding hers. "I knew exactly what I was doing and why I was doing it. And it wasn't because I was looking to hook up with you."

Her body heated at his words, her heart rate kicking up. "So you're on board with building something more, then?"

"I'm on board with building something more with you."

He moved then, walking over to where she stood and looked her in the eyes. "Are we okay, now?"

"Yes. I know you were probably angry the other day, so I'm relieved that you are still here."

"As you should be," he retorted. "I don't commit to just any woman, you know?"

That he should make such a statement after all she had just told him was exhilarating and a little scary at the same time.

"Have you done that before?" she couldn't help but ask.

"No. You'll be my first."

She wanted to ask him why he chose her but satisfied herself with a quiet, "Thank you." Then, before he could speak again, she continued, "Ready for lunch?"

"Yes, please. I'm famished."

Glad of something to do after that weighty conversation, Toni reheated the lasagna and let him make a small green salad when he offered to help. They sat down to a hearty lunch, and when Niall helped himself to seconds, she asked, amusement lacing her tone, "Didn't you eat before you came?"

"No. I slept like the dead for longer than I planned and didn't want to spend time eating when I could be here with you. I knew you'd feed me."

She chuckled. "Well, I'm glad I made as much food as I did. You can have the rest to take home."

"It's really delicious. You cook well. Do you enjoy it?" He looked up at her as he asked, a smile creasing his cheeks.

"Yes, I do, very much."

"What was the first thing you learned to cook?" he asked, spearing another bite of pasta.

"Scrambled eggs. I was nine, and anything requiring more finesse demanded a level of skill I had yet to master." She chuckled at the memory of standing with her mother at her side, breaking the eggs and whisking them before pouring them into the skillet and spinning them into a creamy delight. "I love eggs and breakfast food in general."

"So breakfast for dinner is a thing with you, then?" Something like affection shone in Niall's eyes.

"You know it. Best dinner ever!"

They laughed companionably and Toni's tension eased completely. So she wasn't prepared for his next request.

"Tell me about your ex."

Immediately her eyes shot to his. Why would he ask her that? What did he want to know? And how much should she tell him? Niall didn't seem like the kind of man who would take anything she told him about Randy calmly.

"What do you want to know?" Maybe if she hedged, he'd give her an easy out. There was no way she really wanted to talk about her ex and certainly not with the man whom she was beginning to suspect could be a superior replacement in every regard... if she let him.

Niall's look told her he knew what she was doing, and his reply told her he wasn't having it. "You never mention him. I understand why you might think it awkward to do that with me, but I'm curious about the man you chose to marry. I already know that your marriage was unhappy based on that comment you made about sharing your client's history." He paused, spearing the last mouthful of food before continuing, "How old were you when you married him? Were you always unhappy with him? What happened to change things between you?"

Toni put down her knife and fork and took a fortifying sip of her drink. This wasn't going to be an easy conversation. She never talked about Randy, mostly because it sometimes triggered memories she wished to avoid. Maybe that's where she needed to begin the telling, so Niall would understand how difficult it was for her. Who knows? Maybe he'd even tell her to forget it. She could hope, though she realized it was a faint one. And really, didn't she need to be totally honest with the man she wanted more with? If he was committing to being with her, surely he needed to know what he was up against? And surely he would be there for her when she fell apart?

CHAPTER 8

N iall watched Toni struggle with how to begin the story he was forcing her to tell him. He wondered if maybe he should let her know he already had some of the details. He'd thought about it a lot while he'd been away, following the trail of the man she had been married to, and he had decided that he had to ask her, that she needed to come clean with him.

He hadn't told her anything specific about the work he did, so she couldn't know he was working with others to bring down the man who had once been her husband. But he needed to know the full story, and she had to be the one to tell him. He didn't want her thinking he was stalking her, and he wanted to see if she would be honest with him, especially after the fallout from their first time together in bed.

To say he still wanted her would be an understatement. His every waking thought, when he wasn't focused on work, was of her. What she was doing, who she was with, how she was feeling, especially once he discovered who she was to his target. He let her have her moment to settle herself. He would come clean once she had shared her story. If things didn't go the way he wanted them to, at least he would have heard it all and would have a better idea about the man they were hunting.

He couldn't shake the niggling suspicion he had that Richards was back in England because of Toni, and he'd be damned if he let any harm come to her. No matter what happened between them, she was his to protect from now on.

"I don't talk about Randy because if I think about him too much I have nightmares," she began, avoiding his gaze.

Part of him wished he could tell her to forget it, that it didn't matter, but he knew he'd be lying if he said those words. It did matter, and though he was sorry to have to put her through the trauma of a retelling—because nightmares suggested trauma—he held his silence and let her speak.

"I was twenty-one and a half when I met Randy," she began. "Fresh out of uni, spending time with my parents in Trinidad. He was sufficiently older than me that it made my parents anxious about a relationship between us. But I ignored their fears. I was a grown woman, and I knew what I wanted. Who I wanted."

Pain etched a rigid line across her lips as Niall watched her. Whatever she was thinking about, it hurt deeply. He ached to reach out and had to clench his fists to keep from touching her. He waited, silent and concerned, for her to continue.

"Randy was a charming man back then. I don't know about now. He seduced me as much emotionally and mentally as physically, and within six months we were married. I loved that he lived in England because it meant I could return and live away from my parents' obvious disapproval of him and of our relationship."

"I imagine that that was difficult for you," Niall murmured. She didn't seem to have a bad relationship with her parents now.

"It was, but I figured it was worth the pain of being on the outs with them to be in with this gorgeous man who made me feel like I was the most important thing in the world to him, the operative word being 'thing.' Because it soon became clear that I was more like his most prized possession rather than his life partner."

Niall heaved a heavy breath. Many abusive men treated their wives like possessions. He was very much afraid he knew exactly where Toni's story was going.

"He wanted children, but I never conceived and after a couple of years of marriage, he began to get testy about it. I suggested that we get fertility tests done but he refused, saying we just needed to try harder. I said maybe we should stop worrying about it and it might happen on its own. After a third year, he got angry. He said I was working too hard and that was why—because my body was worn out."

"Why would he refuse to get tested?"

"I don't know. Maybe he knew they would show he was the problem? He wouldn't want that... he's way too arrogant to be happy being a dud."

Did that mean she knew that she wasn't the problem? Had she had the tests done to satisfy herself? If that was the case, she could still have his babies... if he wasn't shooting blanks. He caught himself and rolled his eyes inwardly. *Not where your head should be right now, lad!* Niall could almost hear his dad's voice chastising him for his wayward thoughts at that moment.

"How long were you married to him?" Niall asked, to get his mind back on track. He already knew the answer to that, but he needed to ask it anyway in order to ask the "why" part of the question.

"We were together for seven years altogether. But the abuse didn't start until the fourth year. By that point, I had suggested adopting, fostering kids, even having a surrogate, anything to give him what he wanted, but he refused everything."

She closed her eyes, squeezing them so tightly shut that Niall could see the wrinkled skin around them. *More pain*, he thought, and clenched his fists harder.

"What did he do to you? And why did you stay with him?" These were hard questions. Niall was sure they were some of the same kinds of questions that she'd been asked before.

"Shame. I couldn't face my parents and tell them I'd given up on a marriage after four years because my husband was upset that we didn't have any kids. Then guilt. I kept thinking that maybe it was my fault, that I should stop working so hard, and take him up on the offer to stay at home and be a good little housewife. And then fear, when the abuse became more than I had ever thought he would do, and I was afraid he'd kill me if I tried to leave."

Niall stood up abruptly, knocking over the chair he'd been sitting in. He couldn't stay seated a second longer. He had to work off the rage that had built up in his veins as Toni related her story. When she flinched, he swung around to face her, an apology on his lips.

"Sorry, love. You okay? I didn't mean to startle you." *Of course she's not okay, you idiot! You just took her back to the days of her misery with that arsehole.*

"Y...yes, I'm fine. Are you?"

Something about her question struck Niall as ludicrous. Why wouldn't he be fine? He wasn't the one reliving a horrendous life with an abusive partner.

"I'm fine." His voice came out all rusty and growly. "Go on. What made you leave?"

She sighed. "At first, the abuse was just verbal. He said I was secretly taking birth control tablets, that that's why I couldn't get pregnant. The first time he hit me, he apologized immediately and said he didn't mean it, that he'd never hurt me, all the usual stuff."

She stood up and went to get wine from the fridge. Niall got two glasses and after she poured, he took his and they both sat down again. Each sipped quietly, then she spoke again.

"I actually left him twice," she began, "but each time he found me where I was and persuaded me to go back with him." She shook her head. "I can't believe I was such a fool. How could I have believed he really loved me when it didn't take long each time before he'd hit me again?"

"The last time when I left him, I did it after he left for a business trip. He hadn't just slapped me that time, he'd beaten me badly and left me, thinking I'd still be there when he got back. He said I was cheating on him, and this was to teach me a lesson, that I was his and no one else would ever have me." She took a big swallow of her drink and then went on. "I called Karen, who told me to call the police while she called my parents. She knew it would be easier for me to talk to strangers than to my mom and dad... shame is a powerful deterrent."

This time, Niall didn't resist the need building in him to offer her comfort. He reached across the table and took her free hand.

"I am so sorry, love." He remembered that there was a mention of a charge of domestic abuse brought against Richards in the files they had. He made a mental note to check the police report regarding the case more thoroughly. "What happened with the police?"

"The court issued an injunction, but he has missed every court date that they've set."

Niall wasn't surprised. The man was wanted for far greater crimes than wife beating, though that wasn't nothing, either. To show up for that smaller crime would leave him open to arrest for the larger ones, and however crazy Randy Richards was, he was no fool.

"I only called them because I knew if I didn't Karen would do it for me, and I couldn't handle any more humiliation," Toni was saying. "They came, I gave them my statement, and they took me to A&E. After they released me, I went back to get my things and moved out. My parents called and asked if I needed them to come and get me. I told them no, that I'd see them in a couple of days."

"I'll bet that didn't go over well with them, especially not your dad."

A mirthless chuckle escaped her. "You'd be right about that. But my parents know me well enough to know when to push. I went to stay with them and filed for divorce while I was there. He tried calling me, so I had his number blocked and then I got rid of the old phone. My mother got me in touch with someone in the program at Hope House, and once they'd helped me figure out new housing, and I'd been in therapy for a while, I knew I needed to start over."

"Is that how you found the job at Hope House, then?"

She nodded. "I had been a counselor in a clinic before that, but after the last incident, I sent in my resignation. I told them I had a recurring health issue that I had to deal with and couldn't manage it while working."

She drained the wine in her glass and poured herself more. Niall watched her, aware that after the story she'd just told him, she needed the alcohol to dull the pain he had made her dredge up. He hated that she had had to rehash all that hurt but now that it was out in the open, he could be there for her when the memories became over- whelming. And she had helped him add to his tar- get's profile, which was all to the good.

"Have you had any contact with him since the divorce?"

"No. I changed my phone number and I paid to make it so I can't be found in address searches online. Also, I keep a low profile online. I don't do social media and you will really only find me through my job with Hope House, which maintains a website and has employee profiles."

Niall wanted to tell her that her ex had the means to find her if he chose to, but he thought better of it. Now wasn't the time to add to her stress by scaring her with that news. He'd let a little more time pass before burdening her with that. Still, he realized he'd need to figure out a way to watch out for her until the bastard was apprehended. He'd have to discuss that with the others.

Now he needed to distract her, give her something to look forward to, to replace the unhappy recollections of her past. Maybe this would be a good time to extend the invitation to Sunday dinner again. His parents kept asking when they would have the chance to meet his mystery woman, and even if his heart skipped a beat at the thought of introducing her as such, after that conversation in which he'd basically told her he was committing himself to her, it was probably high time he took her for a visit.

He changed the subject. "Do you have any plans for next weekend?"

It would give her—and him, if he were honest—time to get used to the idea, to prepare mentally for what could potentially be awkward for both of them. Despite her apparent outgoing demeanor, the real Toni hid behind that public affability.

He didn't want to scare her away, but he knew that spending time in the country with his family would go a long way toward relaxing her.

"No. I had been planning to visit Karen in Birmingham, but she's off to hang out with her Dutchman for the weekend."

Ah! He assumed that Karen's Dutchman was the older chap she'd been having supper with that first evening that he'd seen her at the pub.

"Well, my parents have family dinner every Sunday, though we usually spend the day with them and have lunch, as well. They live about an hour away from London and it's a quiet neighborhood. You'll like it."

"Have you told them about me?" she asked, as if she suspected that he'd done that.

"Only that I've been seeing someone. They've been asking to meet you, and I thought that you might like to make another happy new memory, like the ones you made when we spent the day at Jake's place."

A real smile creased her lips. "That sounds lovely, even if I'm worried about meeting your parents."

It suddenly occurred to him that she hadn't said anything about her in-laws. Had she met them? What had her relationship been like with them? He couldn't ask that now, of course, but he hoped when she met his parents it would be with fresh eyes, with no preconceived notions about how they would be. He knew his parents would be welcoming, especially because they sensed that she was becoming important to him.

"I'll make my mom's special bread pudding to take with me," she said. "It's rich and custardy and chocolatey. I'll bet you'll love it."

"My dad has a notorious sweet tooth, so I'm sure he will love it more than all the rest of us."

"All the rest of you?" She cocked her head in curiosity.

"I have two younger sisters, Zoe and Phoebe, and both are married with children. Though they aren't twins, their husbands are. It's a long story."

Toni's expression had grown faintly alarmed. "So, it's not just to meet your parents, it's to meet your whole family?"

"They're really quite harmless," Niall told her with a chuckle. "I promise you."

"Do I have to glam up?" she wanted to know next. "I mean, Surrey is known for its wealthy enclaves, and I don't want to look out of place when I get there."

Niall burst into delighted laughter. "You're funny. My family is well off, but we're not royalty, for heaven's sake. There's not even a Lord or a Lady among the lot of us, so you won't have to stand on ceremony. And you should bring a bathing suit... there's a pool, and the house is right on the water, so we can go boating instead, if you prefer."

"That all sounds quite lovely, Niall. It's like you're never out of great date ideas."

Niall loved the admiration in her voice. "I pay attention to my dates, so that I can keep things fresh and creative," he informed her with a smile.

They cleaned up after that, standing side by side at the kitchen sink. She washed and he dried and when everything had been put away, he turned to her and said,

"Any more *Call the Midwife*?"

Toni grinned at him, clearly pleased that he remembered. "I see I've made a convert out of you. There are whole new seasons of it for you to watch. Come on."

He stayed to watch two episodes, wishing he didn't have to leave. His protective instincts had been awakened by the story about her ex, but he wouldn't let her know about the niggle of worry that had grown as she had told her story. He'd talk to Jake and his dad to see what they would suggest. His instincts were not usually wrong, and something told him that Richards being back in the country had something to do with his ex-wife.

Before the Monday morning meeting, Niall went over the personnel files that they had been given for Richards, searching for information about the domestic abuse case. He found it in a single line of text that merely corroborated what Toni had told him. He'd need to have that case trail followed and their National Crime Agency—NCA, for short—contact would also need to be told about Toni. He didn't like it, but she could become an important part of their investigation and she would need to be protected, given her history with Richards.

"What's on your mind, son?" his father asked as soon as the weekly meeting ended and the others had returned to their own assignments.

"I know where Richards' ex lives and what she does for a living."

Neither his father nor Jake said anything, though he saw when his friend put two and two together and figured out what Niall would say next. His eyes widened, but he kept silent.

"She's one of the social workers at Hope House. It's a shelter for abused women. She lives in Bexley." He pointed to where he had added it to the digital file.

"And how do you know this?" His father eyed him speculatively.

"She's the woman I've been seeing."

A heavy silence fell in the room, broken only by Niall's equally heavy sigh.

"Have you told her what you're working on?"

His father had a right to be concerned about Niall's keeping the integrity of their work intact by not sharing it with people not directly involved in the search. And now that Niall had become compromised because of his personal involvement with someone even tangentially related to the case, his father had to ensure that all confidentiality was maintained.

"No. I asked her about him when I got back, but I didn't tell her what I suspected. She was distraught, as you can imagine, and I didn't want to add to her burden, especially since I hadn't informed you all yet."

"Do you think she knows what he's been up to, what he's been doing since they were married?" Jake asked.

"No. As far as she knows, he's only wanted to answer the domestic abuse charges."

His father stood up and went to the window overlooking the street, his hands thrust deep into his trouser pockets. Niall recognized the pose... Alistair was in deep thought, and Niall couldn't blame him. This was a thorny problem.

"Is there anything else we should know?" his father asked, turning back to face them.

"Nothing concrete," Niall said. "But my gut is uneasy. Why is he back? Does it have anything to do with her? My gut says it does, but I can't imagine what it could be."

"She'll have to be told, son. And if you're right and he's back because of her, she may be in danger. Have you mentioned any of this to NCA?"

"Not yet. I figure it will be better coming from you."

"You know they'll want you to distance yourself from this case now, if they determine that she's useful in any way, don't you?" His father's tone was heavy.

"I won't let them use her like some kind of bait," he said vehemently.

"I don't think you have any say in what she chooses to do once she's been given the facts, Niall." Alistair's tone was stern. "And you know NCA will do what they want whether we approve or agree or not. We have no jurisdiction in the matter." He resumed his seat at the head of the conference table, clasping his hands before him as he continued.

"And perhaps you're right that I should be the one to inform them. If you go in all hotheaded, you'll only make things worse. We need to be able to stay on this, which is what I presume you want if this woman means anything to you. And judging by your little outburst just now, she does."

Niall couldn't deny it, but he didn't like how neatly his father had tied things up. He really had no rights where Toni was concerned, and it behooved him to remember that.

"NCA already has eyes on Richards' place. Given the circumstances, Jake, your new assignment is surveillance of Ms. Larson. We can't assign that to you, Niall, for obvious reasons. I'll call Locksley at the Agency and update him."

Jake stood and sketched a brief salute before leaving the room with a quiet "See you later, Niall." He closed the door quietly and Alistair immediately spoke up again.

"When are you going to bring the young woman to Sunday dinner, Niall?"

Why wasn't he surprised that his father had gone there? Niall shook his head but answered, knowing his father would be pleased with what he had to say.

"She's agreed to come next Sunday."

"Excellent! It's just a pity that we will be meeting her with this heavy cloud hanging over her."

"I think she'll be too busy being overwhelmed by all of you to give too much thought to Richards. Speaking of which, when are we going to tell her?"

"I'll have an answer for you by the end of the day. In the meantime, let's see if we can follow the breadcrumbs to where he will be next. Intel only says another auction will happen within the next four weeks and still nothing more concrete as to where, either. But there have to be clues in the data about what he's doing here and we're just missing it. Also, maybe put out some feelers to our contacts across the pond. Maybe they're hearing things we're not that might help us. This must be some large-scale event that he's planning if he's here and being so cautious. The last auction we broke up had well over thirty girls between the three venues."

"Or it could be one of those high-priced exclusive ones with younger people that requires far greater security."

"That might also be the case. Rich, dirty old men and amoral twats won't spend good coin on sex slaves if they're not guaranteed absolute safety from scandal and arrest. And greedy men like Richards will bide their time and make the investment in advanced security because the expected payout will more than cover the initial setup cost."

Alistair was right, of course, and the thought sickened Niall. But he was grateful that he was at least still being allowed to work behind the scenes on the case. So he couldn't be part of any protective detail assigned to Toni, but that didn't mean he wouldn't spend as much time as he could with her. He trusted Jake to watch her back, and he'd make damned sure no one laid a finger on her when they were together.

CHAPTER 9

I t was Wednesday evening, and Niall had come over after work. He'd called her earlier to say he needed to see her, but something about the way he'd said it told her he wasn't thinking about passion and romance.

"Toni, have you heard anything from your ex recently?" That was how he began the conversation.

"No. I haven't. Why?"

He sighed heavily and took her hands in his. She could tell he was trying to find a way to say whatever was on his mind, which told her that what he had to say wasn't going to be good.

"He's involved in some heavy stuff, love. A lot of law enforcement agencies are looking for him."

Understanding made her eyes widen. "Including your company?"

"Yes. And we're concerned that he may try to contact you."

"But why? We haven't spoken to each other since the divorce. He doesn't know anything about me anymore."

Should she tell him about the note that had been hand delivered to her job hours after Eric's death? It hadn't been signed, but she had known who sent it. It had let her know that he'd been watching her. She had forgotten about that, had buried it in the back closet of her mind, until Niall's news had brought it all flooding back. It didn't matter now, did it? Obviously Randy knew where she worked, at least, but she wasn't going to switch jobs and give him the impression that he had the upper hand. She wouldn't give him the satisfaction.

Did he know where she lived, as well? She wanted to believe that him finding out where she worked had been a stroke of luck, that she was safe, because she had never heard from him again. But then she remembered Eric and the eerie note he'd received with the flowers. Was Randy stalking her again? The thought filled her with fresh anxiety.

Niall was speaking again. "I have no evidence of this, but I think him risking being here has something to do with you."

Her eyes widened, and her fear must have shown in them because Niall pulled her close, holding her protectively.

"I won't let anything happen to you, love," he vowed. "I promise."

She wasn't worried about herself, but how did she tell Niall that without telling him about Eric and what happened to him? And if the police didn't think there was anything to it, why would

Niall? She had no evidence that Randy had had anything to do with Eric's death, nothing but her gut feeling about the coincidence of it all and the notes he'd sent, the one with the flowers and the one to her. The detectives had said that without physical evidence of his connection to them, like fingerprints, and no signatures on the notes, there was not enough to bring charges against him.

She wouldn't let anything happen to Niall if she could help it, either. And his being with her might make him a target. Maybe that's why Randy was back? If he was still having her watched—the thought made her shudder—he would know she'd been seeing someone, and that possessive streak that she'd thought was sweet when they'd first been together now showed itself to be what it really was... a psychopathic obsession, a deadly jealousy.

Many of the women who came to Hope House had been with men who displayed the same kind of behavior. Some had even made it clear that they would get rid of anyone who tried to take what was theirs. She owed it to Niall to tell him about Eric, if she wanted him to be safe, but she also didn't want to look like a fool, thinking too highly of herself, if it wasn't really about her.

What if she was wrong? What if Eric's death had actually been an accident? What if that note was from one of Eric's exes and not from Randy? Surely there was a world in which Eric had a jealous ex-lover who would rather see him dead than with another woman, right?

"There's something else I need to tell you," she said finally. The moment of truth had come. "You asked me a few weeks ago if I had had a significant other since my divorce and I said no. Well, that was only a half truth."

She couldn't look him in the eye as she made the admission. She didn't want to face the disappointment or anger that she might see there.

"I met someone two years ago and we started dating. His name was Eric Stanhope, and he was a veterinary technician and civilian dog trainer. He sometimes helped us find service dogs for some of our clients at Hope House. That's how I met him."

Consciously bringing Eric back to the forefront of her mind was not as painful as she had imagined it might be. Instead, there was a simmering anger at Randy for what she was sure he had done and a deep frustration in knowing there was nothing that she could do about it. She tried not to give in to the fear that was threatening at the thought that he might try to hurt Niall.

"Go on."

Apparently, she had gotten lost in her thoughts. "Sorry." She cleared her throat. "We had been seeing each other on and off for a couple of months, and I was beginning to wonder if he and I could make a go of things." Taking a sip of wine, she continued. "He'd been telling me in the last few days before … his accident"—why was it so hard to say the word? He was dead, for heaven's sake!—"that he felt like he was being followed. But whenever he turned around to look, he didn't see anyone who looked suspicious."

When she sighed heavily, Niall prompted her. "What happened?" His tone told her he knew that things hadn't ended well.

"The morning of the day he was killed, he opened his front door on his way out to work and found a bouquet of red roses with a note that said, 'Ain't love grand? Enjoy it while you still can.' He called me and asked me if I had sent it and read me the note. I said no, of course, and he said he'd take it to work anyway. It'd brighten up the waiting room, he said. He never made it."

Niall moved closer, taking the wine glass from her and pulling her into his embrace. "What happened?" he asked again.

"He was run down as he was crossing the road from the parking garage where he left his car every day. The paramedics tried to save him, but even after they got his heart started again, he died in A&E in triage."

"How did you find out about it?"

"He had me as the person to call in an emergency. He didn't have any family living here."

"Oh, love, I'm so very sorry for your loss. It must have been so difficult for you."

Toni savored Niall's comforting words and feather-light kisses, realizing with a start that the one thing she hadn't had when Eric had been killed had been someone to comfort her in this way. Her parents weren't in England at the time, and since she had never mentioned him to them, they didn't know that he was important to her. None of her colleagues knew that they had been dating, and Karen hadn't come to live in England yet.

Her younger twin brothers, Brian and Christopher, had only found out when they'd come by to see her because she hadn't been answering their calls. And there wasn't much that they could do with her suspicions, even though she had shown them the note that Eric had been clutching in his hand when he died. She'd been alone with her grief, despair, and rage.

"What did the police say?"

"That the note only had my and Eric's finger-prints, that the flowers had probably been bought from a street vendor since there was nothing on the notecard to identify a particular florist, that the message was odd but gave them nothing to go on that would help to identify the attacker, and that my suspicion that it might be my ex was not evidence they could use to build a case against him."

Niall pulled away to look at her. "Why do you think it was him?"

"Because I got a note at work that afternoon asking how my lover was, and telling me that there was nothing I did that he didn't know about." She shuddered at the memory. "It wasn't signed, but who else could it have been? And how did he even know about Eric, unless he'd been watching me all the time when I thought I was safe from him?" Even now, the idea made a frisson of fear slither through her.

"Did you tell the police?"

"Yes. I took it to them, but only my fingerprints were on it and no other DNA. They said the same thing again. Without anything other than my instinct to go on, they didn't have enough evidence to do anything about it."

"They're right, love, but I'm glad you told me. It always helps to have a full picture when we're on the hunt." He paused, then asked, "Did you like Eric a lot, then?"

That wasn't what she'd expected him to say next. She looked up at him quizzically. Was he asking that because he was jealous? He wasn't stupid enough to be jealous of a dead man, was he? Not that he had any reason to be. She was only interested in him.

"We were just beginning to see each other. He was a nice enough chap, and I did like him. I wouldn't have gone on repeated dates with him if I didn't. But it wasn't a grand passion or anything like that. It wasn't even really passion at all. We were just companions."

"Companions? Was it a platonic relationship, then?"

How honest should she be? She didn't owe him any explanations about her love life before they met, but she also didn't see the merit in hiding who she was. If her relationship with him was to grow and thrive, she would need to be honest and open with him all the time. And she was expecting the same from him.

"Friends with benefits," she told him.

She wanted to add that they had only slept together a few times, but she didn't want Niall to think she was trying to explain away her life or make excuses. She had nothing to be ashamed of and she wouldn't let him or anyone else make her feel self-conscious about her decisions.

At first, Niall didn't respond except with a noncommittal "Okay." Then he added, as though the thought had just occurred to him, "Have there been any other men like Eric since then?"

Was he asking for himself or for the investigation? Would it always come back to that? Her hesitation must have tuned him in to her concern because he added quickly, "I'm only asking because if they were also somehow targeted, it would give us some kind of pattern to follow."

Okay... so for the investigation. It should relieve her because the last thing she wanted was another possessive man trying to micromanage her life. So why did she feel that curious curl of disappointment? *You can't have your cake and eat it too, Toni. Either his interest is healthy and reasonable or it's not.*

"No. You said yourself I haven't been celibate since the divorce. I told you that I did a lot of serial dating, but I haven't tried for a relationship since Eric." She left "until now" unsaid because she wasn't so sure it would remain true after her revelation. She hadn't felt safe to try again, until now.

"You're a clinical social worker, Toni. If a woman came to you exhibiting these behaviors, what would you think?"

Thankful for the change of subject, she answered readily. "I'm not a doctor, but I would assume the person has abandonment issues and may have suffered rejection by people she loves. If she's obsessed with someone, she may try to do things to help her feel more in control of the situation. It's a dangerous mindset because it can lead to violence against the person she loves or against anyone attempting to get close to that person."

The silence after her answer was heavy. Did he understand the danger he was in if Randy was actually psychotic? She had never shared her suspicions with anyone other than the police and now Niall, but perhaps she should have talked to the psychiatrist who worked with Hope House clients in need of his special skill set. Maybe he would be able to give more insight into what might be going on in Randy's mind. She didn't want to think about him any more than she already had.

"I'll see what I can find in the case file about the note. I would assume someone made a note of it, though I don't recall seeing it."

He stood up and Toni stood with him. "Thanks for seeing me on such short notice, Toni. And don't worry. I won't let any harm come to you."

"But what about you?" She couldn't help the worry that seeped into her voice. "I can't bear to think about what he'll do if he knows that you..."

"I'll be fine, Toni. Trust me. I managed to survive a war overseas. I'm sure I'll be okay at home."

He walked away to the front door and when she trailed behind him, not even a little bit consoled by his confidence, he turned back to say,

"Are we still on for Sunday? I think it will be more fun if we spend the day rather than just show up for dinner. We have a pool, and the house is on the river so we can also go boating if you'd like."

Relief swept through her. He was still interested. "As long as your parents don't mind a stranger invading their privacy for more than a couple of hours, that sounds lovely."

"They can't wait to meet you," he told her, a smile that reached his eyes lighting up his face. "It'll be fine, you'll see."

She tried to return his smile. "I hope they won't be disappointed."

She accepted the kiss he leaned in to give her, letting him distract her with the tenderness and the fullness of it.

"One more thing." His eyes grew serious. "No more secrets, okay?" When she nodded, he said, "Good. Sweet dreams, love. Lock up after me."

Sleep didn't come easily that night. Her mind was a flurry of thoughts ... about Randy's reappearance, about Eric's death, about Niall and her feelings for him, about Sunday in the country. When had her life become such a whirlwind of activity and emotion? She didn't like feeling out of control, but there wasn't much she could do about it, aside from live in the moment and enjoy the time she'd been given with Niall. God only knew how long it would last.

"Are you ready for this?" Karen asked Toni three days later.

They were on a video call so they could catch each other up on the latest happenings in their busy lives.

"To meet the entire McLaren clan, you mean? Heck no, but I don't really have a choice, do I? I mean, I do, but why would I refuse to meet his family when I want to be with him and he's away so much?"

She held up a light blue dress because the call was also to get Karen's help in choosing what to wear.

"What do you think? Is this too casual?" The dress was knee-length, sleeveless, and low-cut in front and back.

"Maybe not for a first time meeting. What about that peach-colored linen dress that you bought the last time I was there? You can pair it with those kitten-heeled coral sandals. A sunhat and big dark glasses and you'll be rocking the country set vibe. You can take along a summer cardigan in case it gets chilly."

Toni went in search of the items and then remembered that Niall had said they had a pool. She withdrew the two bathing suits she owned and held them up next. One was a two-piece affair in a rich red, the other a one-piece in color-block red and white.

"They have a pool and Niall suggested I might like to swim. So, which of these?"

The red suit was a bikini, with high cut leg openings and the top was tied with a bow in front, accentuating her breasts. The color block one had crisscross back straps, cut-out sides, and a wrap front. Both were very flattering to her figure, but she wasn't sure she wanted to show up to the McLaren pool in a bikini. Silly, she knew, but there it was.

"Take the one piece." Karen advised her. "I know you and you're already fretting about wearing the bikini."

Toni nodded. "Okay. I have to go. Time to get dressed. The bread pudding is almost ready. Thanks, girlfriend. I'll let you know how it went when I get home later."

"I'm glad you had the talk with him. It's so much easier when you're both on the same wavelength, you know?"

"It really is. Talk soon, K!"

Once she'd hung up, she went to check on the pudding. It was coming along nicely. Fifteen more minutes should do it. She'd be ready by then since she had already done her makeup. When the timer on the stove dinged, she picked up her hat and slouch bag checked to make sure her sunglasses, tablet, and wallet were in it along with sunscreen and a beach towel—in case she decided to go for a swim—and lip gloss, and walked out to the kitchen.

Putting her bag on the table, she took the bread pudding out of the oven and let it sit on a trivet on the counter to cool a bit. She hoped that they would enjoy the dessert, and she would suggest they reheat it so they could have it with ice cream. Should she have Niall stop so she could get some from Sainsbury's? She knew the grocery store carried French vanilla, which would be perfect with it.

Recognizing how nervous she was, she slowed her breathing and reminded herself that she and Niall were friends, that they'd been intimate, that he wouldn't put her in any situation that he didn't think she could handle. And he had said his family was harmless. The thought made her smile.

The buzzer to the building startled her, but she went to let Niall in and then clasped her hands together, waiting by her front door for his knock when he got to her flat. When she opened the door, his eyes widened and he stepped past her without waiting to be invited in, pushing the door closed and backing her into it.

"Good morning, beautiful!" His breath was warm on her cheek before he kissed her on each one, then pulled back enough to look her in the eyes. "You look good enough to eat. Did you pack a swimsuit?"

Toni nodded, apparently having lost the ability to form or voice words. She tried to keep hold of her emotions, but the anxiety that had been slowly burning beneath the surface all morning made her tremble instead when he leaned in to kiss her lips.

"You taste as good as you look," he informed her when he withdrew after a soft, tender kiss. "Ready to go?"

She nodded again, then cleared her throat. She really needed to speak words. She had things to say, after all.

"Will you carry the dessert out to the car for me, please? It's on the kitchen counter. It's a little warm, so be careful."

He followed her into the kitchen and pulled a kitchen towel from the oven door handle, folding it and using it to carry the warm Dutch oven out to his car. He rested it on the top of the car so he could help her into her seat, taking her bag and placing it with the pot on the back seat.

"Comfy?" He turned to her as he buckled his seatbelt.

"Yes, thanks."

She was calmer now, though she was still buzzing from his kisses and his attention to her. She could get used to a man who treated her like she was irresistible, like she was precious to him.

"Can we stop at Sainsbury's on the way, please? French vanilla ice cream goes well with this dessert."

"We'll pick it up closer to the house," he promised.

She smiled her thanks and tried to relax. Today was supposed to be a fun day. She hadn't had one of those in a while. It was way past time for some joy.

CHAPTER 10

T he drive to Niall's parents' home took almost an hour, but Toni didn't mind. It gave her time to settle herself, to prepare for meeting a lot of strangers who only knew that Niall was seeing her. Despite his reassurances, she couldn't help but fret about his family's reception. She was thankful that Niall didn't try to fill the silence with conversation, instead tuning the car radio to a classical music channel. The music was soothing and beautiful.

She let her mind wander as they zipped along the motorway, inevitably landing on the news Niall had given her when he'd come over to see her on Wednesday evening after work. He had brought dinner, and after they'd eaten and cleaned up, he had led her into the living room and told her that Randy was back.

She shook her head. Today was not the day to worry about that. Niall had told her she was safe, and he and his team were all ex-military men who knew how to protect themselves. She was going to enjoy the time she spent with him today and not worry about things she had no control over anyway. She had better things to fret about—how ironic was that!—like whether or not his parents would like or approve of her. She would figure out what to do another day.

"I can feel you worrying."

They had stopped at Sainsbury's and Niall had just got back into the car with the ice cream. He reached out and pulled her hand over his thigh, squeezing it comfortingly. "What can I do to help you relax?"

The thought that popped into her mind immediately was so X-rated that Toni gasped, causing Niall to glance at her.

"What?"

She didn't answer him immediately. What was she going to say? A hard ride would do the trick? She would absolutely not think about riding Niall, not now, minutes away from his family home. She didn't need to show up aroused with no chance of relieving the sexual tension.

"Nothing. Just an errant thought."

Niall's chuckle made her skin heat up with awareness. "Errant, huh? What if we could run with it?"

Trust him to know exactly where her mind had gone! "There'll be none of that, thank you very much. I don't need to be distracted by your... by anything you may be thinking of doing. So, stop it, please."

She pulled her hand away to prevent him from trying to follow through on his question but realized that she wasn't as nervous as she'd been a moment ago, that in fact, she was relaxed.

"You're pretty sneaky, aren't you?" she asked with a smile as he turned onto a long driveway between two stately gates that swung open at a touch from the remote control above his visor.

"I don't know what you're talking about," he quipped, but the grin on his face gave away the lie in that pronouncement.

"Of course you don't," she replied, shaking her head at his teasing. "Thank you, anyway."

He glanced at her again as he drove around to the side of the rather imposing house that appeared after a few hundred yards.

"You're welcome. Come on. Let's go in."

They left his car in the garage, and he led her through the door into the kitchen where he deposited the Dutch oven on the stovetop. Then he took her hand, raising it to his lips.

"Come meet my family, love."

Toni tried not to grip his hand tightly as she accompanied him into a large, sunny room that overlooked a beautiful and expansive garden. Two older people were sitting next to each other on a weathered leather sofa sipping tea and watching something on the widescreen television mounted on the wall.

"Mum, Dad, we're here."

Niall's parents turned at the sound of his voice, both resting their teacups back on the saucers on the coffee table and rising to their feet with huge smiles on their faces. Niall introduced her.

"This is my friend, Antonia Larson. Toni, my parents, Alistair and Felicity McLaren."

"How lovely to meet you, Ms. Larson."

A tall, slender woman with high cheekbones, an aristocratic nose, and lush silver tresses that fell softly to her shoulders, Mrs. McLaren extended a hand and Toni accepted the handshake with a smile in return.

"Thank you, Mrs. McLaren. And please, it's just Toni."

Mr. McLaren stepped up next to his wife and also shook her hand. "We've been waiting a long time to meet you," he said, "so we're very pleased that you were able to join us today."

His effortless military bearing, still very evident despite his advanced years, was almost intimidating. His salt and pepper hair was still cut military style, like his son's, and his sharp eyes and high cheekbones gave his face an elegant attractiveness that his son had also inherited. His shoulders were still broad, and he was almost as tall as Niall.

"I'm happy to be here, sir," she replied, feeling the weight of his gaze.

He was watching her closely as if he were trying to find the answer to some puzzle in her face. She had the sense that he could see right through her very soul if he wanted to, and that she would never be able to hide anything from him if he was determined to find it. Apparently, his age had not diminished his absolute authority. She couldn't imagine any of his children getting away with much.

"The others are out in the pool. I hope Niall told you to bring a bathing suit, Toni."

"He did, yes."

Now that his mother mentioned it, Toni recognized the sounds she'd been hearing as she'd walked into the room as laughter and high-pitched squeals. Oh, yeah... Niall did say his younger sisters were married with kids. She had forgotten that tidbit of information, so she was glad she'd chosen the one-piece suit.

"Niall, please show Toni to the guest room so she can change. We'll serve lunch on the patio after you've both had a swim."

They walked back the way they had come, turning just before the kitchen to walk along a short hallway. Niall led her into a large bedroom.

"I'll come back to get you in about ten minutes. Will that be enough time for you?"

"Yes, thank you. Please let your mum know about the bread pudding, okay?"

"Will do, love."

Niall stared at her for a long moment in silence, then turned away, saying, "Ten minutes, then."

He seemed almost flustered, and Toni knew it was because he was feeling the same pull of attraction, the same need to touch, that she was feeling. She nodded, determined to help him control the desire arcing between them. Neither of them could afford to appear before the rest of his family in a state of arousal.

She changed into her swimsuit and pulled the coverall over her shoulders, glad she had chosen the longer one that would hide her body from his eyes for a little while longer. She was just pulling the beach towel and sunblock from the bag when he knocked again. Taking a deep breath to steady herself, she opened the door. His eyes darkened as he took her in from head to toe and back up.

"Come on," he said, his voice hoarse. "You can leave the towel. We have enough for everyone."

He turned sharply away as if he couldn't bear to keep looking at her. If she didn't know any differently, she might think he hated the sight of her. The kick to her gut told her that that was far from the case, though, and she reveled in the knowledge that he was as tied in knots as she was.

The rectangular pool had an eight-foot deep end with a diving board where two lanky boys and a younger girl were lined up waiting to dive off. Two women, one very pregnant, and a man with a shaved head in shorts and a wildly floral shirt, lounged lazily, watching the children play. One other man was treading water, apparently the designated lifeguard in case any of the children needed assistance.

Toni walked a step behind Niall, who stopped by two unoccupied loungers to one side of the pool. He dropped the towels he had picked up on one of them and stripped out of the black t-shirt he'd been wearing. She had done her best not to ogle his muscular lower half, including the tightest, roundest, most coin-bouncing arse cheeks she'd ever seen on a man, but now she was confronted with the sight of him in body-defining black swim trunks that barely managed to disguise the size of one of his most appealing muscles.

She hurriedly pulled her eyes away from his body, not needing any reminders of just how well-endowed he was, and not wishing to advertise to anyone how much the sight of him aroused her. Turning, she dropped the bottle of sunblock and the floppy sun hat onto the other chair and reached up to pull her coverall over her head, hating how self-conscious she felt knowing that more than one person was watching her. Niall's groan when she revealed her swimsuit was low enough that she didn't think anyone but she had heard it, and it sent flares of heat zipping through her.

She didn't dare look him in the eye, especially when he said, "I don't know about you, but I need to cool off." She knew he wasn't talking about being hot from the sun and she had to agree that cooling off sounded like a really good idea. "Coming?"

She looked up then and his eyes were blazing out at her. "I just need to put on some sunscreen first. I burn easily," she babbled nervously.

She turned away again to pick up the bottle and opened it, pouring some of the milky liquid into her palm and coating her arms.

"Here, let me help you." Niall didn't wait for her to agree but poured some into his own palm and added, "Turn around so I can do your back for you."

His hands shook ever so slightly, and the thrill of her effect on him made her brave enough to say, "Need me to do your back?"

"No, thanks. I'm fine."

Monosyllables seemed to be all he could manage as he stepped away from her.

"Come on. Let me introduce you to the others."

Niall didn't look at her but turned to walk away and Toni followed him over to where the women lounged.

"Zoe Buchanan," Niall indicated the very pregnant woman, "Phoebe Buchanan, and John Buchanan, this is my friend Antonia Larson. Toni, these are my sisters and one of my brothers-in-law. John is Zoe's hubby."

John stood up and shook her hand, and the women smiled at her, murmuring a quiet hello.

"Welcome to McLarenland," Zoe added with a chuckle. "Don't stand on ceremony here. We're all a little bit crazy, but we've learned to tame it in public."

Laughter greeted her words, and the children, who had all dived in by that point, climbed out of the pool along with the other man and strolled over so they could be introduced.

"Richard Buchanan," he pointed to his other brother-in-law, "his sons Joshua and Joseph, and John's and Zoe's daughter Sarah. Guys, this is my friend Antonia Larson."

Richard, who was the mirror image of his twin, except for his buzz cut hair, grinned widely and opened his mouth to say something, but a sharp look from Niall seemed to quell the impulse. He smiled at her instead, apologizing for the wet handshake.

"Nice to meet you," he said.

The three children all smiled shyly and went back to the diving board, ready to get back to their fun. Niall walked over and stood behind them, waiting his turn and then almost recklessly throwing himself into the water after them. The children yelled their glee as his dive sent water washing over them. Sarah swam over to him as he surfaced, shaking his head, and wrapped her arms around his neck while her cousins jumped on him, doing their best to dunk him. They laughed as they all struggled together to push him under and Niall's wide grin made her heart melt.

"Not a diver?" Richard asked, still standing beside her.

"Not even much of a swimmer, actually," she admitted, "but I love the water and it's been quite a while since I've spent any time in it that didn't involve an umbrella and galoshes."

Richard's rich laugh soothed her suddenly jangling-again nerves. "Don't worry, my Phoebe isn't much of a swimmer, either, but that has never stopped her from having a good time. Go on, have at it. Niall will make sure you're okay."

Leaving Toni to make her own way into the pool, he went over to where his wife lay and leaned down to plant a soft kiss on her cheek. She smiled up at him as Toni slid into the water, pushing away from the side and swimming to the shallow end. The sight of their affection raised melancholy feelings that she couldn't handle alongside all the other emotions already swamping her. She did a few slow laps, wearing herself out, enjoying the pleasant coolness of the water on her skin. It had been too long since she'd had a swim, and she was tired when she finally stopped.

Flipping onto her back, she closed her eyes and floated for a few moments to calm her breathing, then jerked when she bumped into a hard body. Her eyes flew open, and she floundered as she turned with an apology on her lips. The words died on her tongue at the sight of Niall up close. Water droplets studded his broad shoulders like fat diamonds, and his eyes blazed with need, his water-logged lashes hiding them after a fleeting moment.

"Sorry. I…"

"You're fine, love," he said, his eyes on her lips. "Mum says lunch is ready."

She returned the favor, licking her lips at the sight of his full lips slightly parted as if to get more air into his lungs.

"Toni, behave!"

She smiled and swam away, needing the water to cool her heated skin. Thankfully, the food had all been placed on a long table at the other side of the pool, giving her time to dry herself a bit and pull the coverall back over her body. Clearly, she had to do her part to help Niall keep control of his libido, and if covering up her wet body would do the trick, she was all for it.

The children went first, their grandmother supervising their choices while their mothers were waited on by their husbands. Niall approached her, his eyes still dark with heat.

"What would you like? We've got Scotch eggs, sausage rolls, cheese sandwiches, potato salad, and fairy cakes. To drink there's lemonade, beer, or water. Help yourself to whichever you prefer."

"I'll have whatever you're having," she decided.

He turned away without responding and she picked up a bottle of water and a cup with ice before returning to her lounge chair and stretching out on it, closing her eyes again and enjoying the pleasant warmth of the afternoon sun. Though it was early summer, there would no doubt be a harder chill in the air once the sun went down.

Niall returned with two plates laden with food. "I thought we'd share," he said, "since you opted to eat what I eat."

Sharing, as Toni discovered, actually meant Niall mostly watching her eat while he guzzled water as though he had an eternal thirst.

"You haven't eaten a thing so far," she pointed out as she bit into one of the cute little cheese sandwiches. "You won't get full by watching me eat, you know."

"I'm fine," he said. "You eat up, though. I know my mum makes the best Scotch eggs, and the fairy cakes are to die for."

"So, Toni, Niall tells us that you're a clinical social worker at Hope House. That sounds like it can be a very challenging job."

Mrs. McLaren's voice broke into the bubble that Niall had enclosed them in, and Toni turned to see his mother watching them with a small smile on her face. Glad of her darker skin tone so the blush heating her skin would be harder to see, she swallowed the food in her mouth and answered honestly.

"It is, but it's also endlessly rewarding. I really love it when my clients find their way through to a better, brighter way forward. It makes the difficult times worth the effort."

Realizing that she was gushing—talking about her work always sent her into rhapsodies about the joys of the job—Toni shut herself up by stuffing her mouth with the rest of the cheese sandwich she'd been eating. A quiet chuckle next to her brought her eyes to Niall, whose eyes shone with knowing amusement.

"Oh shut up!" she hissed at him, daring him to laugh at her openly. He turned his face away, biting his lips to keep the smirk hidden.

"I had a friend who passed through Hope House a year or so ago," Phoebe said. "She had nothing but good things to say about it. Maybe you know her? Jennifer Raines?"

The name sounded vaguely familiar, but if she had been one of the clients whom Toni had worked with herself, she would know it for certain.

"She wasn't one of my personal clients, but her name does sound familiar. Perhaps I did the intake for her. I'm glad to know she's doing well."

Glad of something to do besides drowning in awareness of the man sitting next to her, Toni listened as the others talked about subjects as random as the boys' next soccer matches and Sarah's advancement in her martial arts program. She had learned that the boys were nine years old, and that Sarah was six.

She let herself wonder why it had taken Zoe six years to have a second child and why Phoebe had stopped with the twins. There were all sorts of reasons for their decisions, but it gave her something to do other than focus on the electric charge that crackled between her and Niall, no matter what she did to try to control it. Maybe she should ask what they did for a living... she knew how to have a conversation after all. She had been properly socialized as a child.

"How far along are you?" she found herself asking Zoe instead. Starting with "Where do you work?" felt awkward.

"Six months," Zoe answered. "And in case you're wondering why I look like a house, I'm having twins." Zoe chuckled and her husband grinned at her.

"I can't imagine how you feel," Toni commented truthfully.

When she had first been married, she had dreamed of having children, but as the years went by and she didn't conceive, she'd given up hope, even when she thought it might have been Randy who was the problem and not her. After the divorce, she had refused to even think about the dreams she was giving up to protect her heart. Now, watching Zoe Buchanan beam with joy as she talked about her pregnancy, offering up an explanation for the six-year gap—miscarriages—Toni felt a stirring of something akin to envy.

Tamping it down ruthlessly—what did she have to complain about, after all?—she asked if Zoe had had to take time off work. No better way to start that conversation and no better time than now.

"Oh, I took a year off when we found out," she said, reaching for her husband's hand. "And since the doctor prescribed modified bed rest, it made the decision easier."

"So, what do you do when you're not carrying babies to term?"

"I was the office manager for John's company. He's a tech whiz and we're constantly busy."

"Was? You're not going back?" Niall asked the question before Toni could think of a diplomatic way to do it.

"Yes. We agreed that it made more sense for me to stay home with the children, rather than work and hire a nanny because I know me, and I won't do both well."

"Making sacrifices for our children is what shows the caliber of parents that we are," her father chimed in. "Your mother did the same thing when you girls were born, even though I tried to dissuade her."

He turned to look at his wife, whose smile lit up her whole face. "It wasn't a sacrifice, dear. I loved every one of those years I spent being a stay-at-home mum. And it isn't as though I never went back to work," she added. "By the time you girls were in secondary school for a year, I knew I could deal with working part time and being there for you both. I was glad that I did what made me happy."

"And anyway, there's nothing wrong with being a stay-at-home mum, is there? Any more than there's any special merit in being able to work full time and be a full-time mother," Phoebe chimed in. "Everybody's experience is different, and we shouldn't feel guilty for choosing the path that makes us happy."

Toni got the feeling Phoebe was talking about herself somewhere in there, but that was definitely not a question she could ask. The silence that followed Phoebe's statement felt too loud. Toni asked a question, feeling uncomfortable and needing to de-escalate the tension.

"Have you chosen names for the babies yet?" she asked.

"No. We're just making a list of the ones we like best. We'll have names by the time they're born."

The conversation moved on to the names and Toni drifted again, closing her eyes and letting the sound of the voices wash over her. It was peaceful back here. Between the birdsong, the murmur of voices, and the warmth of the sun, Toni was lulled into a doze only to wake with a start when Niall's voice said in her ear, "Come on. You can doze in the guest room out of the sun, love."

Toni opened her eyes and sat up quickly, looking around her. The men were still there, though they were now sitting around one of the tables under a huge umbrella. She felt a lick of embarrassment.

"Sorry... I didn't mean to drop off like that."

"There's nothing to apologize for. My sisters and my mum have all succumbed to the sun. They went in a minute ago for a nap." He turned to the men and added, "I'll be back in a few. Save me a beer."

CHAPTER 11

B ack inside the guest room, Toni dropped the bottle of sunblock into her bag and turned to find Niall in her personal space. The door to the bedroom was wide open, but he didn't seem to know or care as he pulled her into his arms.

"I need this. To tide me over until we can be alone without other people close by."

The kiss was slow and intense, singeing every one of her nerve endings, causing a quaking to begin in her belly.

"You're too damned sexy for your own good, you know that?" he murmured, stealing another quick kiss. "And for mine."

Another kiss, this one deeper, hungrier, hotter in every way. Toni held onto his arms, knowing that if she wrapped her own around his neck, as she was sorely tempted to do, she would forget where she was and ask for things she couldn't have in his mother's house.

"Bloody hell, Toni!" His voice was hoarse. "I've been a good boy all day, and I still can't have what I want." He kept peppering her face with kisses.

Toni chuckled, her earlier embarrassment forgotten. "What makes you think you'd get what you want, anyway?"

A shadow darkened his eyes when he raised his head to look her in the eye before he blinked and then asked, "Would you make me beg?"

"No." Her denial was immediate. She didn't need him to beg, even if the idea of Niall begging her for his release made her whole body shiver. "No, you wouldn't have to beg."

They gazed into each other's eyes for another aching moment before he dropped his arms and stepped back, his expression neutral once again.

"There's an ensuite bathroom with a bathrobe and everything you need for a bath or a shower, in case you want to do that now. I'll knock when it's time to dress for dinner. Have a nice nap."

Before she could reply, he turned and walked out, closing the door behind him with a sharp click. Heaving a heavy sigh, she took her things into the bathroom, pausing briefly to admire its pretty sunny yellow and lavender colors, the royal purple rugs and towels, and the pretty floral curtains at the window. After she showered, she pulled on the white bathrobe that was neatly folded on the counter by the sink and went back into the bedroom, leaving her swimsuit to dry over the towel rail.

The bed was deeply cushioned, dressed in peach and cream bed linen, and she sank into it gratefully, feeling heavy sleepiness wash over her. She hadn't realized how tired she was. A nap would be just the thing to restore her balance and settle her emotions. She should set her phone to alarm... she'd get up to get it in a minute.

"Toni! Wake up, love." A warm palm cupped her cheek, followed by the press of soft lips. "Dinner will be in half an hour."

Niall helped her to sit up, and she pulled the robe around her more snugly, but not before he got an eyeful of her lush female flesh. Her skin warmed as he moved his eyes up from her chest to her mouth to her eyes. She could see the hunger in them now. He wasn't hiding it, but she could also feel the restraint in the tension in his hand where he still held hers.

"Did you have a nice nap?"

She swallowed. "Yes, I did. Thanks." She looked him over and saw that he was already dressed in the dark slacks and cream shirt he'd worn to get her earlier. "Am I late?" she asked in a sudden panic.

"No, love. You're fine. Just come out when you're ready." His eyes wandered to her lips again. "I want to kiss you so badly, love. Just one. Please?"

His tone held a plea she couldn't ignore. She leaned up this time, offering her mouth to him and he took it, sucking on each lip before sending his tongue plowing into her mouth to take what he wanted. The kiss turned wild as Toni let herself go and demanded satisfaction for the longing she'd been carrying with her all day.

"Darling, we've got to stop. I can't show up for dinner with an unrelenting boner."

Toni licked her lips and smiled, running trembling fingers over Niall's lush mouth. "Go on, then," she said. "Let me get dressed."

He nipped her fingers, sucking the middle one into his mouth for a heart-stopping moment before releasing her and getting to his feet.

"I'll come to escort you to dinner," he said. Consulting the elegant and expensive gold watch on his wrist, he added, "In twenty-five minutes."

Then he was gone again. Toni hurried, spending the most time on her makeup. Although she knew the McLarens were comfortably informal, she still didn't want to keep them waiting, and she wanted to look good enough to be with their son, even if that was not something either of them had discussed.

When the knock sounded this time, she opened the door immediately. Niall looked her over appreciatively.

"As gorgeous as ever," he told her, and extended his arm. "Come on."

The others were already in the dining room when they arrived, and everyone looked very different, but still informal so she didn't feel out of place. The dining table seated twelve, which meant there was one empty place. Toni sat next to Niall, between him and Sarah, who was next to her dad so he could presumably help her with the meal.

A rack of lamb, a roast chicken, and a ham as well as more potatoes and veggies filled the table. Once Mr. McLaren said grace, the men set to serving their wives again. Toni watched in fascination as they effortlessly filled the plates with food, and only when every woman at the table had been served did they serve themselves. She loved it, but she wouldn't begin to eat until Niall's plate was full.

"Not hungry?" he asked, catching her watching him.

"I am, but I'm waiting until you're ready so we can eat together."

She didn't register the silence at the table until Niall looked at his mother. Toni followed his gaze and saw the other woman's warm smile directed at her. What was that for? She looked questioningly at Niall, who only said, "It's nothing, love. Eat up. You don't want the food to get cold."

Everything she put into her mouth was delicious. "This is really good, Mrs. McLaren," she said after taking a bite of the lamb.

"That's Phoebe's contribution, my dear. It is good, isn't it?"

"Very." Toni turned to Phoebe, whose cheeks were faintly pink. "This is great. Did it take a lot of time to do this?"

"Not really. And thank you. I enjoy cooking. It relaxes me when I'm feeling stressed."

"That sounds like a great way to unwind," Toni murmured with a smile.

The talk of food continued as they ate, and when it was time for dessert, Toni did the honors. The pudding had been in the warming oven so it was ready to serve, and Niall added a scoop of ice cream to each portion that she plated. The compliments came almost immediately, making Toni's chest warm.

"This is truly a delight, Toni," Mrs. McLaren said.

"It's decadent," Phoebe added. "You must share this recipe with me."

"I will," Toni promised, smiling widely.

The boys both asked for seconds, and once Phoebe gave them permission, Toni gave them the last of it and watched in amusement as they scraped their plates clean a second time. She insisted on helping clean up and Niall helped as well, and combined with the children's help, the dining room and kitchen were set to rights in no time.

"What would you like to do now?" Niall asked as they walked back into the living room. The television was on, but no one seemed to be watching it.

"I'm fine with whatever everyone else does."

She was curious to see the family dynamic after dinner on a Sunday evening. When she was a little girl, after dinner on Sundays was reading or board games time. No one watched television unless something special was happening that the adults wanted to watch, and bedtime was always early for everyone. She could almost hear her mother saying, "Start the week fresh with a full night's sleep" when they grumbled about going to bed by nine.

"It's every man for himself," Niall told her. "We just do whatever it is we want to do in the same space. Being together is important to us, even if we're not all sharing the same activity. We're like pack animals in that way... we always need to be together when we're together, if that makes sense."

"That sounds pretty sweet," she replied. And it did.

She ended up playing Scrabble with his sisters and his mum while the men got noisy over Monopoly. The children watched television, and the whole atmosphere in the room was cozy and warm. She held her own against the others, though she wasn't the overall winner. It amused her to see how competitive the sisters were, and she mentioned it to Niall as they drove off behind John's car.

"Your sisters are intense, aren't they? Cutthroat competitors at Scrabble, for sure!"

Niall laughed. "Always have been at everything they do together. I'm surprised they didn't get into it about the special merits of their way of cooking whatever. Maybe they were being on their best behavior because you were there."

Toni chuckled. "Well, their control snapped over spelling and plurals." She turned to look at him as he turned onto the road. "I had a really lovely day, Niall. Thank you for inviting me. You have a wonderful family."

"Thank you. I'm glad you enjoyed your day. I know they liked you as well. And Mum likes your manners."

Toni frowned. "My manners?"

"She liked that you waited for me to begin eating. She's old-fashioned like that."

"That was for me," she protested, "not because I was trying to impress anyone with my good behavior. I just wasn't comfortable starting alone since you and I were together. If that makes any sense."

Her voice trailed off, but her heart picked up its pace when he reached for her hand and raised it to his lips before placing it on his thigh.

"It makes sense, love."

She didn't realize that she had dozed off until the car stopped at her block of flats, and she woke up with a start.

"I don't know why I'm so drowsy," she said, faintly embarrassed.

"Sunshine and good food are like the good drugs," Niall said, chuckling. He followed her into her flat, closing the door behind him and pulling her into his arms. "I'll be busy this week, so we may not be able to see each other again for a bit. I want you to know I'll be thinking of you in that sexy swimsuit, probably at the most inopportune moments."

Toni laughed, burying her face in his chest. "Shut up!" She looked up at him then, a smile on her lips. "I will admit that your body in those swim trunks was quite delightful to look at, too, especially when you were wet from swimming."

"You like me wet, huh?" He leaned in and pressed a kiss to her lips. "I like you wet, too."

She knew he wasn't talking about swimming this time and she hid her face in his chest again, her shoulders shaking with laughter.

"Look at me, Toni," he demanded, pulling her face up with a finger under her chin. When she complied, he continued, "I'm putting you on notice, love. I want to make love to you and soon. So, I need you to let me know when you're ready to go there again for real. I won't lie and say no rush, but I will do my best to keep holding onto my patience, for you. I think you're worth temporary blue balls."

When would she truly be ready? She thought about that as she got ready for bed and as she lay watching the shadows on the ceiling, she realized that she very well might be now. There were no more secrets between them, and he still wanted to be with her in every way. That meant she could trust him with her heart because he wanted her despite her past. Now all she had to do was find the right time to let him know that she trusted him completely. That time came on Friday.

"Please, have a seat, Mrs. Cole," Toni said to the battered woman standing across from her on Friday morning. "I'm so glad you came in today, and I'm really pleased that you involved the police this time. Where are your children now?"

The bruises around the woman's eyes and elsewhere on her face were painful to look at. Toni tried not to cringe as she watched her sit carefully in the armchair in front of the desk. Emily Cole had refused assistance the first time she had been referred to Hope House, but Toni had known she'd see her again. She hadn't expected it to be so soon, though. *Really, Toni? Soon relative to what?*

"I sent them with my oldest to their gran. I have to call her in a bit, but I just wanted to make sure I could stay here?"

The fear, the uncertainty, the hope that all bled through in her client's words and voice struck Toni in the heart like a blow.

"I'm sure we'll have room for you, Mrs. Cole, don't you worry. And tomorrow, we'll get moving on the legal side of things, beginning with an emergency injunction. It will cover both you and the children. Have you given any further thought to what you're going to do going forward? You'll have to make a more permanent decision if you don't want to repeat these steps later on."

Toni didn't have it in her to suggest divorce more openly. She'd been where the woman sitting in front of her was and she knew how hard it was to choose the hard road that ripped her away from the person she had thought would be her world for the rest of her life. It should have been easy, but it hadn't been. The look on the woman's face told her everything she already understood. She wouldn't press her. Her job was to support and encourage, not to coerce, even if that was all she wanted to do.

Once she got the older woman settled, she logged her report, scheduled wellness and mental health visits, contacted the lawyer whose office handled all Hope House's cases, and went on to the next thing on her agenda. Just as she was packing up to leave for the day, after checking to make sure that Mrs. Cole had been offered a place to stay, her cellphone rang.

"Hey, Niall."

Butterflies took flight in her chest. Apparently, they'd taken up permanent residence there since the day she'd met him, and they were keenly attuned to him. The very sight of his name made them flutter giddily.

"Hey, Toni. I wonder, are you free this weekend? Monday is a bank holiday, so it'll be three days."

They hadn't had a moment recently to be alone together so she wasn't going to refuse whatever he was about to propose.

"I am, as a matter of fact. Why?"

"Um..."

It wasn't like Niall to hem and haw. What could possibly be making him anxious right now?

"Is everything okay?"

"Yeah, everything's fine. How would you like to go away with me for the weekend?"

"I'd love that. But why do you sound so tense? Where are we going?"

"How would you like to go to the beach? We could spend some time together, just the two of us, getting to know each other better."

Ohhh! He was probably worried that she'd refuse because she wasn't ready. "I'd like that. I haven't been to the beach in a while, though I imagine the water will still be pretty cold."

"We don't have to go swimming in the ocean. The hotel's pool will suffice for that if you want to get wet."

His voice dropped lower, clearly intent on seduction, reminding Toni of their byplay on Sunday night when he'd dropped her home.

"Or we can go for walks on the beach, if you prefer. And of course there's shopping, a fun fair, restaurants, and shows. There'll be more than enough to do."

"That sounds delightful, Niall. What time shall I be ready?"

"I'll come to get you at nine. Pack something fancy for dinner out on Sunday."

Her mother called as she was packing later.

"Mama! Are you back?"

She had only spoken to her parents once since she and Niall had been together. They had gone off on an eastern European jaunt and she only heard from them sporadically, mostly so she wouldn't worry that anything had happened to them. She loved that they didn't hover, and that they enjoyed their empty nest to the max.

"Not quite yet, dear. Your father and I are going to spend a few days in Scotland before we return."

"Don't you have a couple of cruises planned before you go back to Barbados?"

"We do, and also a reunion with our crew at Mont St. Michel."

Toni sometimes envied her parents their carefree lifestyle, but she knew they had earned it and she didn't begrudge them a second of their fun.

"And how are things with you? We haven't heard much from you in a while. Is everything alright?"

Toni hesitated a moment too long, and her mother spoke again, this time with a note of concern. "Antonia" —she only called her that when she was in full Mama Bear mode – "what's going on, love?"

"Everything is fine, Mama." She should probably tell them about Niall, especially since they'd moved on to spending a weekend alone together.

"What aren't you telling me, dear?" Toni heard a muffled sound, then, "Ron, your daughter is keeping secrets from her parents."

Toni sighed. Her mother always called in reinforcements, a.k.a. her father, whenever she thought she needed the voice of authority to keep their children in line.

"Mary, you do remember that Antonia is a grown woman, don't you?"

"I'm putting you on speaker, Antonia," —Ah, so she wasn't out of the woods yet! – "so you can tell us both what it is you're keeping from us."

"I'm not keeping anything from either of you, Mama," she protested weakly. "It's just that we haven't talked for more than a minute or two in so long, and life goes on, you know?"

"So what exactly is going on in your life that would take more than a minute or two to share with us, girl?" Byron Larson had a booming voice to match his large size.

Toni sighed. Her father always sounded impatient, especially after she married Randy. He hadn't truly forgiven her for ignoring his advice— he called it disobeying him—and she was sure he secretly felt that everything she had suffered since then she had earned through that decision. She knew he loved her in his own odd way, despite the hard line he always took when it came to her. If he didn't care, he wouldn't be angry, right? That's what she told herself anyway.

"I've met someone," she blurted out, not sure there was any other way to say it.

The silence on the other end of the line was so long that Toni began to wonder if the call had been cut off. "Mama? Dad?"

Finally, her father spoke, his voice curiously hoarse. "We're here, Antonia." He never shortened her name, even when he wasn't angry with her. "Are you happy?"

Her heart melted at the question. Her dad wasn't a hearts-and-flowers kind of man by any means, but he was fiercely protective of those he loved. And that the first question he should ask wasn't about the man she'd found but about how she felt told her how much her happiness meant to him.

"Yes, Dad. I'm happy. And I'm safe. He's former military and he co-owns a detective agency with his dad. They work with the CID, NCA, and Interpol sometimes."

"What's his name, Toni?" Her mother's question was much more expected.

"Niall McLaren."

"Another white boy, then?"

The note in her father's voice this time was not quite disapproval, more resignation. He would probably never stop wondering why she couldn't find a Barbadian or Trinidadian to marry, and she had stopped pointing out that there were at least one or two white men from both those Caribbean nations.

"He's not a boy, Dad. He's forty years old." Time to shut this down. "Anyway, that's all my news. I have to go now. I'll be away for the weekend, and I need to pack. Enjoy Scotland and take more pictures. I'll come round for a visit when you get back."

"Bring that boy with you when you do," her father said, clearly ignoring her previous words.

Almost immediately after she hung up, her bestie called. She heaved a relieved sigh. This call was just what she needed after the unexpected tension of the previous conversation. Karen had recently spent a weekend away in Woodstock with her man, and she was thrilled to hear that Toni was following in her footsteps.

"That's not the way it usually goes with us, is it?" Karen quipped with a chuckle.

"True. I'm usually the one leading you into trouble."

"Well, I'm glad this time it's good trouble you'll be getting into."

Toni laughed. "Fingers crossed and all that, right? Anyway, I'll be sure to give you the low down when I get back. Maybe we can compare notes."

"So, what are you thinking, Toni?" Karen's tone grew serious. "Do you think Niall's the one?"

Her parents hadn't asked her that, though she supposed the way she had hurried them off the line hadn't given them time to even think about the question. Thinking about it now, she wasn't sure how she would have answered it had they asked, because even without them knowing any-thing about him aside from what she had told them, they—especially her mother—would have started making wedding plans. And she wasn't there yet and preferred not to fight with them a second time about a wedding that had not even been introduced into any conversation between her and Niall. But she could admit the truth to her best friend.

"He just might be at that. I mean, he ticks all the boxes, you know? He's focused, he's kind, he's passionate, he likes me just the way I am."

"And don't forget he's Mr. Chick Magnet," Karen added teasingly. "Have you noticed that? I mean, do you find other women ogling him a lot?"

"I haven't really, but then I haven't cared to watch anyone else when I'm with him, to be honest. He's an interesting man. Besides, we've not been out in public a whole lot. I suppose I was too busy ogling him myself to notice anyone else."

"As long as you're the only one he's paying attention to, it doesn't matter." Karen sighed. "I'm really happy for you, love. Niall seemed to be a very forthright man when I met him, so if he is still pursuing you, I'd take that as a sign that he's not going anywhere unless you send him off."

"He's already told me he's not," Toni admitted. "It was a bit intense at the time, but although my head says it's really soon after we've met to be feeling this way, the rest of me is all on board with doing this."

It was about time, too.

CHAPTER 12

Toni was still thinking about that as she and Niall drove off the next day. She hadn't told Karen about Randy's reappearance because aside from Niall warning her to keep the information to herself, she knew her friend would worry. Karen didn't know the whole story, but she knew enough to know that Randy was a dangerous man.

"What's got you so quiet?" Niall glanced over at her before turning his eyes back on the road.

"Nothing much." She might as well tell him about her phone call with her parents. "Just thinking about my parents."

He glanced her way again. "Is everything alright?"

"Yes. Everything's fine. They're extending their holiday and taking in a bit of Scotland before coming back to England. And they have more trips and things planned before they go down for the winter."

"Wishing you could be free to roam like they are?"

She smiled. How easily he read her feelings! Even though that had not been her thought in the moment, she did often wish she could fly away at a moment's notice like they so often did.

"I have wished that from time to time, though I hate flying so that would be a challenge for me," she confessed. "But that wasn't what was on my mind just now." She had promised him no more secrets, but how did she broach the subject of her father's response with him without offending him?

"They weren't pleased with your news?" His statement was voiced as a question.

She sighed. "They weren't *dis*pleased. Just..." She hunted for the right word.

"Cautious?" he suggested.

"Yes, I suppose that's the word. Particularly my father."

Niall chuckled. "I can't say I'm surprised. My dad is a bit of a bear when it comes to the girls, as well."

Maybe she could keep the reason her father was cautious to herself. What Niall didn't know couldn't hurt him, and at the end of the day, she was confident that he would win over both her parents with his charm and sophistication as well as the aura of power and security that he wore like a second skin.

"Hey, don't worry. I'll be on my best behavior when we meet, I promise." He grinned at her briefly. "And if your parents are like mine, they've already made demands about meeting me, yes?"

Toni shook her head in amusement. "You understand about parents so well. I've been told to, and I quote, 'bring that boy' when I go to visit them."

Niall laughed loud and long. "Boy, eh? I guess I'll take it since they are your parents so they'll be older than I am." He chuckled again, then asked, "Where do they live?"

"In Edgbaston. They didn't want to move too far away from Birmingham, which is where my brothers and I were born."

"It's a pretty suburb, and Birmingham is a great city," Niall said. "Do you normally take the train or drive there?"

"I always take the train. The motorway is too much for me."

"Just let me know when you're going. As my friend Jake would say, road trips are my jam."

"I'll bear that in mind."

Toni felt light as air, buoyed up by Niall's good spirits and his apparent lack of concern for her father's possible poor reception of him. She needed to learn how to be this carefree. The rest of the way to Brighton was filled with laughter as they sang along to the pop songs on the channel he'd chosen this time. Niall could barely hold a tune, much to Toni's amusement, and he laughed harder than she did at his attempts to sound like Luther Vandross and Michael Bublé.

The hotel was a charming and elegant affair, and as the bellboy escorted them up to their rooms, Toni tried to control the thrill that was bubbling inside her. Once he left them, she walked to the big picture window and let out a muted squeal of delight at the view. It doubled as a pressure reliever since her joy could no longer be contained.

They hadn't done anything other than leave the city and already she was almost giddy. She took several deep breaths to calm herself and turned to find Niall standing behind her, watching her with a smile on his face.

"Happy?" he asked.

"I can't believe how much I am," she said. "Thank you. You knew I needed this. I'm so grateful to you for leaving your work to spend time with me."

An almost guilty look crossed his face then. "Well, I still have to work, but I wanted to give you something to ease your mind."

"Are you going to be working today?" He had figured out a way to kill two birds with one stone and she refused to let his work mar her fun.

"Not yet. Let's go walkabout for a bit, have some lunch, and then you can go for a swim while I do some work."

They spent the rest of the morning walking along the boardwalk before stopping for lunch, which they enjoyed in the open air. Back in their suite, they both changed into swim gear, but Niall took his laptop with him and sat on one of the loungers typing away while she swam lazy laps and floated. They were the only ones there at that hour, which suited Toni just fine. When a few other guests began to trickle in, she got out and went to lie next to where he sat working.

"Ready to go up?" he asked.

"Yes, please. Sun and swimming have done me in, again."

He chuckled and waited while she pulled on her coverall before extending his arm.

"What are we going to be doing this evening?" she asked as they went up in the elevator.

"Do you mind if we have dinner in this evening? I have to be available for a conference call."

"I don't mind if we don't do anything, Niall," she told him. "As long as I don't have to make the meal, I'll eat anywhere."

"Choose what you like from the menu and have them add it to the bill, please. When do you want to have dinner?"

"Six would be good."

"I'll make sure I'm ready for six, then." He put down his laptop and pulled her into his arms. "I promise to be completely free by bedtime, okay? I won't let anything interfere with that."

He winked at her then and kissed her, chuckling when she sputtered against his lips, unable to quell her amusement.

"Typical male," she said. "Nothing interferes with nookie."

He laughed with her, kissed her again, then took a seat at the table and got back to work. Toni made the dinner order and decided to take a shower. She was just setting the water temperature in the two-person stall when Niall knocked and walked in uninvited. His eyes were blazing, and Toni shivered.

"Is something wrong?" she asked, painfully aware of her nakedness.

"No." His eyes roamed over her from head to toe, heating up at the sight of her heavy breasts. "Everything is fine." He stepped into her personal space. "Why don't you invite me to join you? I could use a shower as well."

"I thought you were busy," she protested, moaning when he stole a quick kiss. "Are you feeling dirty or something?"

He groaned at her words, raising a hand to stroke her lips with his thumb. "I always feel dirty around you, love." He raised an eyebrow, waiting.

"Would you like to join me in the shower, Niall?" she asked obligingly, tickled by his teasing.

"I thought you'd never ask," he quipped, taking a deeper kiss.

"What about your work? The conference call?" She really didn't care, but someone had to be sane and responsible.

"I told Jake I was going to take a shower, to give me half an hour." he quirked a brow at her as he stripped out of his clothes. "Which means we don't have a lot of time for shenanigans now."

Toni laughed. None of the men she'd been with had ever made her feel comfortable enough to laugh when they were intent on seducing her. Niall made it so she was desperate to give him anything he wanted, as quickly or as slowly as he pleased.

"Shenanigans, huh? Who knew you had it in you?"

He wagged his brows and reached past her to test the water temperature. "There are a lot of things you have yet to learn about me, love. Shower shenanigans are just the tip of the iceberg."

He pulled her fully into his hard body and thoroughly explored her mouth. His hands stroked her everywhere, dragging pleasured sighs and moans from her. He strolled his fingers down her belly, squeezing her breasts and pinching each nipple on the way to her woman's mound. Toni opened her legs, weak with desire for him and gasped when he lightly tapped her aching pleasure button.

He lifted his mouth away from hers to ask, "Toni, are you still sure that you want to do this now?"

His question gave her pause. They hadn't slept together since that first time, which she had said had been too soon after they met, and he had agreed to take it slowly. But now her heart and mind were both in agreement with her body, and she was more than ready for him to take her completely, to substitute his fingers for the part of him that seemed intent on branding her soft flesh with its steely hardness.

"Yes, I'm sure."

"Thank God for that!" he whispered fervently before stroking into her wet channel, bending his knees so he could send his fingers up. Once, twice, three times he plunged into her before he withdrew and stepped into the shower stall.

"Come on. Let's get you clean."

Niall washed her flesh tenderly, his touches firm and practical. Then he pushed her back against the wall across from the fall of water and said, "Hold on to me, love."

He picked her up then, keeping her back firmly against the wall, and thrust into her with his hard cock. They both grunted at the impact, and then he was slamming into her over and over, Toni could feel her body weeping for him, easing his way with her juices. She hung onto his neck, pushing back to get the maximum effect of his taking, nonsense words rising to her lips as he made love to her hard and fast.

"Oh, darling woman," he huffed, pausing in his wildness to steal a wet, breathless kiss. "You take me so well." Thrust and withdraw. "I could fuck you forever, love." Thrust and withdraw.

All the dirty words she had ever heard used in a sex scene rushed into Toni's mind as Niall sped up, thrusting deeper and twisting his hips so he could catch her sweet spot on his way in.

"Oh, please, please, Niall!" She was babbling and incoherent.

"Anything you want is yours, baby," he told her as he lit her up inside again and again. "Just don't let me go."

Words became kisses, became groans of pleasure until they both burst the banks of feeling and soared. Her heart raced as her body climaxed, and Niall's hard rod pulsing in release inside her added sparks of electricity to her orgasm.

"Jesus, Toni!" Niall's breath was labored as he leaned into her, his cock still jerking inside her. "Don't let me go, baby!"

"I won't."

She clung to him fiercely, loving the feeling of his softening cock inside her, wishing she could keep him there. When he slipped out of her and helped her to lower her legs, she leaned heavily against him, her face hidden in his neck.

"Toni, are you alright?"

The breath of his words warmed her ear, and the care warmed her heart.

"Yes." She looked up then, meeting his eyes. "I'm more than alright, Niall. I..."

He stopped her words with a deep kiss, sucking on her lips and tongue, nipping his way back inside when she pulled away to catch a breath. She returned the hunger he was still so clearly feeling with her own awakened desire, knowing how deeply she had fallen for the man she still had her arms wrapped around.

She had almost told him just now, but the time wasn't right for that. Randy was still out there, and she would never feel relaxed and worry free until he was apprehended. She had to make sure nothing happened to Niall because if he was taken from her, she didn't know how she would survive this time.

"Come on, love." His voice interrupted her musing. "Let's get you dried off and into bed. I have to get back to work, anyway. Play time is up for now."

He rinsed them both off and helped her dry herself. "Go on. I'll wake you when dinner is here."

After dinner, while Niall took his call, Toni watched more episodes of *Call the Midwife* and then switched to some of her favorite police procedurals. When Niall joined her on the couch, she leaned into him without a second thought.

"Done for the day?" she asked.

"Yes. Would you like a nightcap? Dessert?"

What she would like was more shenanigans, but she wasn't quite ready to be that brazen with the man even now watching her expectantly.

"Maybe just some crisps and a soft drink."

"What would you like to do tomorrow?" he asked.

"I'd like to see all the touristy sights, if you please, and maybe another walk along the beach path this time?"

"We can order a picnic lunch so we can eat on the beach."

"Good plan."

She was ready for some mindless fun, and a day in the sun would help to keep them out of bed. After all, wasn't this supposed to be a getting-to-know-each-other-better trip? If, at the end of it, the only thing they learned was what the other liked in bed, that wouldn't have been the best use of the time, would it?

Not that she minded spending more time in bed with him. Now that she was on board with intimacy that meant more, she craved the touch of his hands on her, the feeling of fullness when he was inside her, the words he spoke that lit her up and made her feel cherished. She squirmed at the thought, feeling Niall's eyes on her as she did.

"Where did you just go?" he asked, taking a long swallow of his drink.

"Nowhere," she answered, giving him the half-truth.

"Are you sure?" He tilted his head, his lips quirked, a look in his eyes that said he didn't believe her. "Because you had a faraway look on your face there for a moment. Remember, you promised no more secrets. So spill, love. Where did you go just now?"

She could see that she'd never get away with anything with this man. She shook her head but answered him anyway. "I was just thinking that if we spent too much time on 'shenanigans'" — she put air quotes when she said it— "it would defeat the purpose of us getting to know each other better."

"Hmm." He scratched his chin for a moment, then said, "In other words, you were thinking about shenanigans, yes? Between the two of us? Somewhere in this suite?" He paused, piercing her with his stare, before adding, with a mischievous smile, "Somewhere else? Do tell, love. I'm game for whatever you want to try, whenever you want to try it."

She laughed. What else could she do? "That last bit is just wishful thinking on your part," she said, not answering his question directly. He was an investigator. Let him figure out the answer.

He stood up suddenly, swallowing the rest of his drink in two gulps, and put the glass down.

"Come here." He held out a hand to her.

When she took it, Toni knew there was no turning back. This was the first night of the next phase of her life, the one where she was happy and safe with someone who saw her as she was and didn't mind. She walked with him to the bedroom, one of her mother's favorite sayings playing over and over in her mind... *There is a God.*

CHAPTER 13

"What's the news?" Niall settled his hips against the desk and waited for Jake to speak.

"Both you and Toni are definitely being watched, but neither man is our target. And since the NCA isn't as concerned about domestic abuse, they won't do anything about it. The murder angle has them looking again, but with nothing concrete to go on, they're mostly leaving that to us to figure out as well."

Niall wasn't surprised. "Anything on the next auction?"

"Next week some time, and not in the UK. So that's now off our plate. The only thing the NCA is focused on now is apprehending Richards because he's been named as a major player in an ongoing human trafficking and sexual exploitation case. And because they know he's back on British soil, possibly after his latest sale, they're looking to score a quick victory and get him off the streets."

Something about the way Jake said those last words made Niall's hackles rise. "What aren't you telling me?"

"They've looked at the intel regarding Toni and want to interview her."

"To what end?" Niall's voice was hard.

Jake shrugged. "I asked and was told that she may be key to finding Richards and disrupting his criminal organization."

"I won't have it," Niall barked, straightening angrily and pacing away to the door and back. "They can't make her put herself in danger."

"You don't have a say in the matter, Niall, and you know it. It will be up to her to decide what she will or won't do for them."

"Then I'll just have to persuade her not to get involved." He sighed, running a hand through his hair roughly. "This is my fault," he said. "If I hadn't given them that data, they wouldn't be trying to use her as bait now."

"Niall, you do realize she's already in danger, right? If that madman escalates and tries to kill her instead of just the man she's with, where does that leave her? You have to give her the chance to do something. Based on everything you've told me, she's not likely to be happy waiting in the wings to hear whether or not you've been run over."

Niall sighed heavily and took up pacing again. "So, we're out of this except to find evidence he's a murderer as well?"

"More or less. Your dad's talking to them now. And if my hunch is right, they'll be contacting Toni before close of business today."

After the best weekend he'd spent in more years than he could remember, this was definitely not the way he'd wanted to spend his first day back at work. He knew that Jake was right. He had no say in the way the NCA conducted their business, nor did he have any control over Toni's actions. Just because they'd slept together a few times didn't mean she would want him to be proprietorial with her. They weren't anything more to each other than occasional lovers, even if all he wanted was to be her only lover for the rest of their lives.

When had that happened? When had he fallen in love with her? And how had he not even noticed it? Sure, he knew he wanted something long term with her. He knew he wanted to be with her alone. But he hadn't thought beyond that to what it meant that he was committing to this one woman. The enormity of the emotion was more than he could handle at the moment, what with the fear for her that he was fighting to control.

"Breathe, my friend," Jake said in his ear.

He inhaled, realizing he must have been holding his breath, or hyperventilating, or both. He didn't really know.

"She's going to be okay, Niall." Jake's reassuring words and his supportive hand on his shoulder helped him bring his rioting emotions back under control.

"We'll see to that, I know," he said, forcing a confidence in his tone that he had yet to feel. But if he said it loudly enough, he'd believe it, right?

The office door opened just then, and his father walked in. Niall knew by the look on his face that what he had to say would not be good news.

"They've called your friend, son, and she's to be interviewed in the morning."

"Does she know what it's about?"

"Not unless you've told her more than you should."

Niall didn't bother to answer that. He was more concerned about what story they had spun to get her to agree to speak with them. He had to prepare her, but how did he do that without giving her information that was classified? Should he invite himself over for dinner and ask her what she had been told? What would he say to her, anyway? She needed her ex to be caught because his freedom was a threat to her peace of mind. She worried that he'd come after Niall, and while she might be right, Niall didn't care about that as long as the maniac didn't change his focus and go after her.

"There's precious little you can do aside from being there to support her, my boy. And even that will depend on whether or not she asks for you to be there with her. You're not a lawyer, and she's not under arrest, so she doesn't need anyone with her."

A long silence followed before his father spoke again. "In the meantime, we have other cases to work on. And there are reports to be completed by both of you." He sighed and spoke to Niall again.

"Try not to worry, Niall. Toni seems to be a sensible young woman. I'm sure things will work out well in the end."

The rest of the day was a struggle for Niall. He tried to finish the backlog of paperwork from the week before, so he'd be able to start fresh on the new load, but he kept going over all he'd discovered this morning. Finally giving up, he saved what he'd been working on, shut his laptop and went in search of his friend.

Jake was on the phone when he knocked on the partially open office door and walked in. He sat down across from his friend and took out his cell phone, hoping to see a message from Toni. Nothing. He debated the merits of sending her one himself, then scotched the idea. She was at work, just like he was, and didn't need to be distracted any more than she probably had been by that call from the NCA.

"Don't do it, Niall." Jake's warning meant he'd finished his conversation and Niall hadn't even noticed.

"Sorry." What was he apologizing for? He shook his head. "I can't focus, so I'm taking a mental health minute or ten."

Jake chuckled. "I can't believe it! We've known each other for how long? And I've never seen you this bent out of shape over a woman. Have you finally figured out that you're head over heels in love with her?"

"What am I going to do about this interview?" Niall didn't answer his friend's question, which he knew Jake would take as an affirmative.

"You are going to do nothing, my man. Wait for her to ask for advice. Don't go in all macho man. That's likely to drive her away. Based on what she's told you and what we can see from the ex's case files, he was a possessive asshole. She's not likely to take kindly to you acting like she belongs to you. You feel me?"

Of course, Jake was right. But how could he just sit and wait, hoping she'd call and ask for his help? He knew she didn't really need him for much beyond the pleasure he could give her, and in other circumstances, he didn't mind that. But he couldn't bear the thought of any harm coming to her because he was hamstrung by her independent streak and his lack of jurisdiction.

"Look, let's finish up here and go for a drink, huh? Maybe you'll feel better with a couple of pints inside you."

It would take more than a few beers to drown his anxiety, but he didn't have a better offer, so he nodded and went back to work. Later, they sat in the pub watching the traffic in and out of the establishment. Niall barely noticed individuals, seeing them more as suits, dresses, tall, short, round, thin, loud, quiet. No doubt Jake was eyeing the women... it was what he did when they hung out together. It was what Niall used to do as well.

His thoughts turned to Toni then, and after his second pint, when there was still no message from her, he ordered a gin and tonic and drummed his fingers on the tabletop. Jake sighed.

"Look, if she hasn't called or texted by the time we're ready to leave, which looks like it will be soon if you plan to avoid having a hangover at work tomorrow, you can call. What you say to her is up to you. I'll go get you a glass of water to wash down your pissy mood."

His cell phone pinged out a message notification while Jake was still at the bar. *Toni!* He read the note twice, relief sweeping through him.

[Toni: Hi. I need to talk to you. Can you call me, please?]

Niall stood up, rattling the glasses on the table.

[Niall: Give me a few minutes.]

He sent off his reply and hurried to the john. When he got back to the table, Jake was sitting there, nursing his own glass of water.

"Toni asked me to call her. I'll be back in a few."

He made his way out to the wide patio where some of the bar's clientele sat drinking and talking. He went to a quiet corner and called her.

"Toni? It's Niall. I'm with Jake at the pub. What's up?"

"Did your dad tell you I had a call from the..." He heard the rustle of paper. "National Crime Agency?"

"Yes. He told me they've invited you down to talk to them in the morning."

"Aside from when I went to the police about Randy, I've never done this before. I was wondering..."

He didn't wait for her to finish, hoping he was right that she wanted him to accompany her.

"I'll go with you, love." He bit the inside of his cheek to stop himself from offering more than she asked for.

"Thank you. I'm to be there by nine, so I'll drive down and meet you there?"

"Or I can come and get you. I'll drop you at work after if you want." When she didn't reply, he added, "Don't worry about it. I'm sure they just want to corroborate the facts to make sure they know everything you do about what happened back then."

"I think they want more than that, though."

Niall tensed. "What do you mean?"

"I think they're going to ask me to help them with more than information."

He had not known how difficult it would be for him to avoid jumping in and telling her not to offer any more help. Everything in him screamed at him to stop her, but he managed to keep it to himself. Instead, he said, "Don't do anything to put yourself in danger, love."

That was the least he could do. It was sound advice and he hoped she would read between the lines and do what he wanted—needed—her to do.

"I'll see you in the morning then," she said, not acknowledging his last statement. "And thanks again, Niall. Goodnight."

"Any time, love. Goodnight."

He heard himself speak the endearment for the first time with the knowledge that she was his love, that it was more than just a common word passed between friends and acquaintances, that it meant more.

"Toni wants me to go with her in the morning, so I won't be in until later," he told Jake, sitting down and drinking the whole glass of water. He needed to be sober enough to drive himself home, which meant he had to hydrate and give the alcohol already in his system some time to settle.

"See? You were stewing for nothing."

"She also told me they want more from her," he ground out.

Jake sighed. "And what did you say to that?"

"I just told her not to put herself in danger. That's a reasonable thing to ask, right?" He wouldn't back down from that.

"It is. Just don't forget that's all you can do or say."

He was still telling himself that the next morning as he drove her to the NCA headquarters. She was quiet, clearly tense, and he didn't want to add to her anxiety by speaking out of turn. He escorted her into the building, and as they made their way to the office where the meeting was to be held, he reached for her hand.

"Relax. Everything will be fine."

She gave him a tight smile and he wished he could loosen her up with some kisses, but this was neither the time nor the place for that. He satisfied himself with keeping hold of her hand until they were invited into the office, and then he just focused on keeping silent. Once she repeated everything she'd told him before, the NCA officer asked her if she would be willing to help them capture their target.

To his credit, the officer didn't tell her the full extent of the crimes for which her ex was being hunted, and Niall breathed a sigh of relief at that. But that was the extent of it. He hated every word that came out of the man's mouth from that point on.

"We don't ask this of you lightly, Ms. Larson," he said, giving her a small smile.

Niall recognized the technique and he hoped that Toni saw through the ruse as well. To them, she was just an asset, nothing more.

"As long as I won't be in any danger, I'd like to help."

Good girl! She didn't say anything more and the agent hesitated. Niall opened his mouth for the first time and asked, "What exactly do you want Ms. Larson to do?"

"We have reason to believe that Richards will be conducting business," he gave Niall a pointed look at that which he understood immediately, "at an auction in a prominent hotel in London this coming weekend. We want to force his hand. If you are correct, Ms. Larson, and your ex is exhibiting obsessive behavior toward you, we think he will be more likely to act on impulse if he sees you accompanied by Mr. McLaren as a guest at the event."

So she wasn't the bait... *he* was. He didn't have an issue with that, but why did Toni need to be there? He asked as much.

"If I'm his target, why can't I go by myself? Why allow her to get anywhere close to him?"

"As you're aware, Mr. McLaren, Ms. Larson has been under surveillance for the last few weeks."

Niall heard Toni's gasp and winced. He'd be hearing about that later, and he'd have to come clean about his part in it. For now, he focused on the agent's words.

"So far, he's been able to evade us because he's been very deliberate and careful with his appearances in public. And this is how he operates, so there are never any surprises. Assuming he's already on high alert, we hope that seeing her with you in the flesh will shock him into taking action himself."

"If you know he'll be there..."

"That's the thing," the man said. "Based on our intel, we have reason to believe he may be there, but it's not a certainty. He's been really cautious and not shown his face in weeks, and if he suspects that he's being set up, he'll bolt. Normally, he doesn't spend so much time in one location because he has seconds to do his dirty work for him. There's another reason he's still in England and if Ms. Larson is correct, it has to do with you. He's less likely to suspect anything if you show up together to a public auction."

"He's also less likely to do anything with her there," Niall argued.

"Agreed, but it could possibly force him to escalate. If Ms. Larson is correct in her assumption, he has had more than enough time to know that you're seeing each other, but he's not made a move against you so far. We want to force his hand."

Toni had been silent as they argued back and forth but finally she spoke, asking a question that made Niall at once proud of her intelligence and frustrated with the agent.

"I'm confused about something," she said. "What function is this that Randy will be attending, and what business will he be conducting that either Niall or I would want to have anything to do with?"

A small, pointed silence followed her question before the officer replied. "Are you aware of what your ex-husband does for a living, Ms. Larson?"

"When I was with him, he was in marketing. He worked in his father's company back then. I don't know anything about him now."

The man's lips tightened, and Niall could guess what he was thinking. Marketing... the best way to hide his nefarious activities, and why would anyone, including his wife, question his frequent evenings out and trips abroad?

"Do you know what his inventory consisted of?" he asked next.

Toni shook her head. "I never asked. Why is that important? What does it have to do with him having Eric killed?"

The officer sighed heavily and looked at Niall, who shrugged and looked away. This was the NCA's game, and he wasn't going to help them play their hand.

"Your ex-husband is, and has been for some time, a major player in human trafficking and sexual slavery, both here in the UK and abroad. He is on our Most Wanted list."

Despite her darker skin tone, Niall saw how Toni lost color at the agent's words. She looked like she was going to faint. He went to her, crouching next to her chair.

"Breathe, love. You're okay. You're safe." He held her hands as he soothed her.

The agent stood and left the room, and Niall pulled her to stand so he could hug her. She was trembling and he hated it. He wished there was more he could do aside from hold her and help her not to hyperventilate.

"Alright?" he asked when she stirred against his chest.

The agent returned just then, before she could respond, carrying a tray with three mugs. Niall released her and she sat down heavily.

"I thought you might like some tea, Ms. Larson."

Toni nodded her thanks and took one of the mugs. He offered a second one to Niall, taking the third for himself and sipping it slowly, giving her time to compose herself.

"I'm sorry that you had to find out this way, Ms. Larson. Our concern is to close down his operations, find and release his captives on British soil, and put him behind bars for his crimes. We're already making some inroads into the first two of these goals. Capturing him would go a long way toward more fully achieving them."

Niall knew the reality was a lot less neat and tidy than that. Men like her ex, as kingpins in their organizations, were never without a backup plan in the event that things went pear-shaped. But he'd take majorly disrupting Richards' enterprise and even shutting down a few of the places where he kept his slaves if it meant Toni could finally stop worrying about what could happen to any man she was with. About what could still happen to him, as long as Richards was at large.

The meeting ended. Toni didn't agree to help, but she didn't refuse, either, which meant Niall would have to try his best to help her choose Option B. He understood that the NCA was beyond desperate to make an arrest, and if they could nab Richards, it would be a coup and a great public relations boon. The agency had been under fire for failing to curb what had rapidly become one of Britain's biggest crime outbreaks. Putting Richards out of commission would be a feather in their cap.

He wouldn't let them use Toni to score brownie points, though. They were the law, dammit! They needed to do their job without involving civilians. And he'd be damned if he let them endanger the woman he loved.

"Do you feel up to going into work, love?"

They were standing outside on the pavement, and he turned her to face him, searching her face for further signs that she was not okay.

"I have two clients coming in this afternoon, and I have a home visit to conduct. I don't have a choice."

"What happens when you're sick?"

"I'm not sick, Niall," she snapped. "Being shocked is not being ill. I have to go to work."

Niall backed off. She was too distraught right now to be logical, and working would probably help distract her from the things she had discovered today. He would see what he could do for her after work.

"Okay. I'll drop you off and come back to get you after."

She didn't argue about that, which he considered a win. In her present frame of mind, anything could make her snap, and he had the feeling she was a force to be reckoned with when she was angry. When he stopped outside Hope House, he turned to her, needing to show her how much he cared and wishing he could do more than hold her hand.

"Call me when you're ready to leave."

"You don't have to do that, Niall. I'll be fine. I can use a car service."

Her voice was stiff, almost cold. She'd had so much thrown at her this morning that he wouldn't be at all surprised if she was feeling out of control. He wouldn't add to those stresses if he could help it.

"Humor me, love," he answered. "Shall I send over a light lunch for you?"

She stepped away from him then, her eyes sharp. "Stop! I'm fine, and I don't need you to send me food or pick me up. I just need a little time, please. Thanks for coming with me this morning. I appreciate it."

She moved away before he could reply, walking to the building with her shoulders squared, the picture of calm confidence. He hoped she'd be able to hold it together and felt sorry for anyone who crossed her today. They were in for a shock as she seemed on the verge of losing her temper. So, he wasn't surprised when she didn't call him after work, nor did she send him any messages. He waited for an hour after she normally left work before deciding he would go to her. Mohammed and the mountain and all that.

He bought a bouquet of variegated blooms on his way to see her, bracing himself for anything that she might throw at him. Starting with what she would no doubt consider her justifiable anger at being watched without her knowledge, he ran down the list of things that could all be responsible for making her irritable. He rang her buzzer before wondering what he'd do if she didn't answer or let him in.

"Who is it?"

As if she didn't know. Niall rolled his eyes but answered in a neutral tone. "It's me, Niall. Let me come up, please."

CHAPTER 14

Niall let go the breath he was holding when the buzzer sounded and before too much longer, he was handing off his peace offering to Toni with the front door firmly shut behind him. She walked away with the bouquet, and he followed her, sitting at her kitchen table and waiting for her to acknowledge him. She placed the flowers in water in a vase and set them on the counter before turning to him, her hands on her hips.

"I think you owe me an explanation, Niall," she said without greeting him. "I thought we had said no secrets."

Ouch! She was right, though he had hoped he would have been able to keep the fact that she was being watched to himself forever. He knew his reasons were in her best interest but given all that she'd had to endure with her ex, and the bombshell discovery she'd made about him earlier, Niall could well understand her ire.

"We set a watch on you the moment we knew Richards was back in town. I didn't tell you because then I'd have to explain all that we knew about him and that wasn't within my purview. We're only assisting as consultants. We have no jurisdiction in this case. We must do as we're told."

She stared at him unblinkingly. "Why watch me, though? He didn't hurt me that time. He went after Eric."

"True, but if he's psychotic, he can decide to escalate. If getting rid of his competition didn't keep you single, then he'd be the dog in the manger. If he can't have you, no one else will. We had to take his unstable mental condition into account."

"Was I supposed to be one of the people he trafficked? Is that why he came onto me?" Her voice was hard.

Ah! It hadn't once occurred to Niall that she might think that, and he could imagine how frightening it must be, even after all this time, and even though she seemed to have escaped relatively unscathed, in comparison to the women who had not and were still suffering. Granted, he didn't have all the facts of the case from the time they'd met when she was twenty-two, and he supposed hindsight was catching up with her now. He answered honestly.

"I don't know, love, though it did occur to me when we first discovered your connection to him. You were still pretty young, and you said yourself that you married him against the wishes of your parents. You fit the profile in terms of age and experience."

He hated to think that she had been an innocent exposed to the likes of Randy Richards, that even if her parents had felt the wrongness of the man, they wouldn't have been able to help her once she left their care of her own volition. He caught the shiver that she tried to rub away by running her hands up and down her arms. He desperately wanted to hold her, but she needed to give him a sign that she was ready to forgive him before he did anything that personal.

A heavy sigh escaped her as she remained standing by the kitchen island, her arms wrapped around her as if to ward off the evil that was her ex.

"Is there anything else that I should know?" she asked next.

No more secrets. That had been the promise he had exacted from her, and as far as the case went, there were none. But there was something he was keeping from her that he needed to tell her. Was this the right time to do that? He didn't really know, honestly, but his heart said he needed to come clean, even as his mind screamed for him to wait, to let her cool off, to be sure what he was feeling was the real deal.

Reason and logic be damned, he had never felt anything like the emotions he felt whenever he was with Toni, whether they were sexual, romantic, protective, affectionate. Her wellbeing, her happiness, had become essential to his peace of mind, He wasn't the same as he'd always been, and if she ultimately rejected him, the loss would be permanently damaging. And it was too damned late to stop that wreck from happening, so he might as well tell her his last secret and let the chips fall where they may.

"I'm not certain that you're ready to hear this," he began, "or that it's the right time to tell you, but I'm going with my gut here, so bear with me."

She remained where she was, but Niall could see curiosity in her expression now. He had never thought about telling a woman he loved her before. The most he had done was decide he was tired of hookups and wanted more. Yet here he was now, about to bare his soul and praying that he wouldn't get his heart handed back to him. Just because they were compatible sexually and she enjoyed their lovemaking didn't mean she was ready for declarations of love. But he had to take this chance. He'd never know if he didn't try.

"I'm in love with you, Toni."

He stopped speaking, resisting the urge to explain himself, to ask what she felt for him, to beg her not to let him go. He waited instead, his heart beating out a rapid tattoo in his chest, fighting to keep his breathing even.

"We haven't known each other that long, Niall," she finally said. "How can you be sure?"

That wasn't a ringing endorsement of his feelings or a sweet reciprocation of his declaration, but it wasn't an outright rejection, either. Maybe she needed to hear how he came to his realization so she could trust her own feelings for him? She had been deceived by a seductive man once before, and even though she was much older and more mature now, he could understand why she might be reluctant to accept that what she was feeling was real. He gave her the words she seemed to need to hear.

"I've never told another woman I love her because I've never felt for anyone else what I feel for you. Truth be told, I've never even had the impulse to commit to another person before you. I was all for the physical relief, nothing for the emotional connection. I hit it and quit it, and I made sure any woman I was with understood going in that those were the rules I played by."

He sighed and stood up from the table then, hating the distance between them, needing to feel her warmth. He stopped in front of her but didn't touch her, still needing her forgiveness and her permission.

"The way we met floored me. You know why I went to that birthday party that you hosted for your friend. I was expecting to leave with Karen and maybe enjoy some fun with her. But the minute you walked into that room, the furthest thing from my mind was being with her because suddenly you were there, and you were everything. Don't ask me how I knew that. Maybe it was love at first sight, though if that's the case, it didn't hit me until very recently."

He wasn't about to confess that he hadn't figured out his feelings until the day before. Some things were best left unsaid.

"Chemistry isn't love, Niall," she said, resignation in her voice.

He felt a flare of anger spark inside him. How dare she try to belittle what he felt for her and make it something trivial like emotionless sex? Fighting the urge to grab her and shake her for that, he clenched his fists instead and bit back the angry retort on the tip of his tongue. He counted to ten, slowly, making her wait for his answer as he had waited for hers. This was too important to mess it up with frustration and misplaced ire.

"I'm forty years old, Toni. I've learned a thing or two since I started down this road. I don't use the word love lightly, believe me. What I feel for you is far more than the need to sink into your flesh, to take you and mark you and make you mine, to have you mark me in the same way. I'm not denying that it is a part of how I feel, but it isn't everything."

It occurred to him then that after the morning she'd had, it was going to be difficult for her to believe him. He knew he was nothing like her ex. Hell, he knew that she knew it as well. But when you've been hurt as badly as she was, it's hard to let go of comparisons, of what ifs, of the fear of repeating the mistakes of the past.

He didn't know how Richards had persuaded her to go all in with him, but if their chemistry had been like his was with her, then her reluctance to believe him now was understandable, even inevitable. He'd just have to prove to her that she meant more to him than a bed partner.

"You're the first female friend I've taken home to meet my family. Even though it was a day jaunt to the country, I deliberately chose to take you there for Sunday dinner. I waited to ask you because I didn't want you to think it was too soon to meet them, but I don't regret it for a second. That was one of the best days that I've spent with my family."

Her eyes said she didn't believe him and her words proved him right. "Even better than a day out alone together in the country?"

"Even better."

He would ignore the prick of hurt that she doubted him, that she entertained the thought that he would lie to her. This was just her fear, her insecurity, talking. He wouldn't hold it against her.

"Whatever you need me to do to prove myself, I'll do it, Toni. You're it for me. Whenever you're ready to move on, I'll be waiting."

There was nothing else to say. He was certainly not going to have his declaration returned to him. Not tonight anyway, and maybe not ever. But he'd done it... he'd said his piece, made his stand. The rest was up to her. He wouldn't regret telling her how he felt because now his heart was lighter. Whatever happened going forward, she knew everything there was to know about who he was, about who he would always be to her.

"I think I'd better go for now. You've had a rough day, and there's a lot for you to process. I'll give you your space."

He reached out and touched her cheek with a fingertip, swallowing the ache of longing that he felt. There would hopefully be time for more after she had had time to think through everything she had learned. He turned to walk away, and she followed him, making his heart sing.

"Get some sleep," he told her as they stood by her front door. "I'll call you tomorrow, okay?"

She nodded. "Okay. And thank you, Niall."

The need to land his lips on hers was overwhelming, but he wasn't going to give in to the temptation. So even though he wasn't sure what she was thanking him for, he said, "You're welcome," and stepped into the hallway.

"Lock up."

He waited until she complied before leaving, knowing someone would be watching her once he was out the door. There was nothing else to do regarding the Richards case. The NCA had things well in hand, and as they'd done what their client had hired them to do, things could go back to normal. He had other cases that he was working, and there were always reports to write.

He slept badly that night, going over and over what he'd said, what Toni had said, how he had left things. What could he do to prove himself? He had no ideas. He just knew that words alone would not be enough for her, and he couldn't blame her. But words were all he had until she gave him something more to do. And he would give her the space she seemed to need, even if it killed him.

He called to check on her the next day, as he'd promised, but Toni hadn't asked to see him, and after three nights of little sleep, and three days of increasingly bearish moods, Niall was ready to tear his hair out. Even his father had lost patience with him, giving him the rest of the afternoon off so he could sort himself out.

"I don't need your moody arse here disturbing the smooth flow of the workplace, boy. Get it together and come back when you've got your head on straight."

Niall couldn't be angry with his dad. He was right after all, so he left the office, spent some time walking to wear himself out before driving home and throwing himself into bed after a hot shower. When he woke up with the morning birds again the next morning, he got out of bed, even though he wouldn't go to the office. He still felt unsettled, and another day off seemed like just the thing.

He'd go for a longer run today, work the anxiety and frustration out of his system, wear himself out so he didn't have too much energy left to fret about his love life. Changing into his running gear, he exited his house and ran off, watching for the few early drivers off to parts unknown for work.

Running with one earbud, because to use two was foolish, he set off along the pavement, stumbling over something on the garden path. He didn't stop to see what it was. He'd deal with it when he got back home. Crossing the street, he made his way down to the river run, a leafy path adjacent to the river. This was his daily route and at this time of the day, the paths were unclogged by other runners and pedestrians, and the streets were somewhat less full of motorized vehicles.

By the time he finished the last lap and was making his way back along the river path, he was pleasantly tired and ready for a long, hot shower. The sun had come up, but the streets were still fairly quiet. Emerging from the river path onto the pavement, something caught his attention. He turned, running in place, trying to decide what had caught his eye. Seeing nothing, he turned again and stepped off the pavement.

That movement stirred in his peripheral vision again and he looked around in time to see the light truck barreling toward him at full speed. He had nowhere to go. He'd be hit no matter what, so he had to decide how much of a hit he could take. In that split second as he was deciding how to turn his body, the van struck. He spun away, hitting the ground with an audible thud. Something cracked, or at least his fuzzy brain thought so before he passed out.

Niall opened his eyes to bright lights and beeping noises and his parents talking quietly to Toni, who had her back to him.

"Toni?" he called out to her. She didn't move. Why didn't she turn around? His eyes drooped. He needed her to look at him. Maybe he was dreaming? Or maybe he needed to speak a little louder? He'd try again...

The second time he woke up, it was to the dulcet sounds of his woman's voice. She was praying. Everything still hurt, especially on his right side, and he was pretty sure he had at least a couple of cracked ribs. But this time, he knew he wasn't dreaming, especially as he heard the words she was speaking to a God he had not spoken to himself in quite a while. He realized he was in the hospital, but how long had he been here?

He listened to Toni to distract himself from his pain and the confusion of not knowing the answer to his question and unwilling to speak himself because he didn't want to disturb her and more because he wanted to know what she was thinking. What was she asking God for?

"These days, I don't talk to you nearly as much as I used to in the past, God, and I know that at least some of that is my fault. And I guess the only reason I'm saying anything now is because you kinda hit me with this new revelation."

Her voice faltered and she inhaled sharply before continuing.

"After Eric, I shut down again. It was the best way I knew how to keep myself safe, you know? I was quite prepared to be single the rest of my life. I have a job I love, a place to call my own, and people who have my back. I really thought I was set. Then you went and dropped that big ole hunk of man there in my lap. What the hell was I supposed to do but fall for him? You did that on purpose to stop me from staying on that other path that only allowed hookups."

He heard her sniffle and his own eyes pricked with tears. They hadn't spoken to each other since he'd called her the morning after her visit with the NCA—had it only been three days?—without knowing exactly where things stood with them. He knew they needed to settle matters between them, but he hadn't known how to start until now. Because now he knew that she loved him, too.

She was still praying. "I'm not ashamed of how I've lived the last two years... well, maybe a little bit." Niall smiled at her frank words. He wondered idly if God found it as funny as he did. "But Niall made it so I can't imagine ever doing anything like that again. Which is a pain if he doesn't wake up. You got me into this damn pickle, so how about you get me out, huh?"

Niall's heart squeezed in his chest, and the tears he had been struggling to hold back welled again in his eyes. He swallowed and willed them away before any could fall. When she had found out that she was being surveilled to protect her from her ex, and that Niall had kept it from her, she had been understandably angry with him. And he had been so very afraid that everything they'd been building would come crashing down around his ears.

He was glad that she hadn't put herself in danger to help the authorities, but he had been careless with his own safety and had gone ahead and done the very thing guaranteed to get him in trouble. He should have known better than to be so reckless about his morning workout routine, given what they knew about her ex. And he knew that she would try to protect him, but dammit, he wasn't a weakling, despite where he currently found himself.

She was the one with no experience in these matters and yet here *he* was. He didn't know what he would have done if anything had happened to her, so he could only imagine how she must be feeling to see him lying helpless, wrapped up in bandages with an IV bag delivering pain medication into his battered body.

Now, though, it seemed he had been given a second chance to get his dream, to keep the woman who had stolen his mind from the first moment they'd met and who had taken over his heart in short order after that. He spoke quietly, wanting to preserve at least a little of the peace that she wanted.

"Toni." When she turned her head he added, "Hi."

Her smile was sad. "How are you feeling?" Worry creased her forehead.

"Groggy and aching but okay. All my bones hurt, but I'll take battered and groggy-but-alive over dead, yeah?"

He didn't miss the shudder that she tried to hide by standing. "I'll get the nurse. They said to call them when you woke up. Don't go anywhere."

He appreciated her attempt to lighten the mood, but even with the headache and his throbbing right side, he knew there was a lot they needed to clear up. Were they finally going to find a way forward after the misery of the last three days? How long had he been in the hospital, anyway... had it been one day? Two? That would mean they had been on the outs for more than three days. And what *about* him and Toni? Would he ever feel certain of anything again where she was concerned? What if she was still angry with him?

"Ah, Mr. McLaren, you've returned to us."

A nurse's cheerful voice interrupted his musings and he smiled wanly as she took his wrist to check his pulse rate.

"How are you feeling?" she asked next.

"Cloudy and gray with a chance of rain," he said, then felt foolish for the comment. He didn't know why he had said that. Maybe he had a concussion?

"We've alerted Dr. Morrison that you're awake, and he'll be with you shortly." She took his temperature next, then checked his blood pressure on his good side. "If you're thirsty, you can have a few sips of water, though we urge you not to have anything for a bit, if you can avoid it." She noted his stats on the mobile computer she had rolled in and then looked him over one more time. "Rest, Mr. McLaren. You'll be with us for at least a couple of days more."

CHAPTER 15

O nce the nurse left, Niall turned to look at Toni, who sat quietly staring at her hands. He had the sense that she had been using the nurse's solicitous questions to keep some kind of barrier between them but he was having none of it. They'd been close before her areshole of an ex had thrown a spanner in the works. Not that he was exempt from all blame. He had gotten his feelings hurt because she'd been trying to protect herself from being hurt again.

He'd need to remember that going forward. If they were to be together, he'd have to accept that she was independent and capable of handling her own affairs. He had to trust that she was not rejecting him if she questioned his actions, and to accept that she would need to protect him as he protected her. It was only fair.

"We need to talk." She flinched and Niall gripped the sheet tightly with his good hand before continuing. "It's not your fault, Toni. You didn't run me down to try to kill me."

Her eyes when she turned them to him for a moment clearly said she didn't agree with him. He wanted to hold her and kiss away every doubt she had, but he wasn't going there again until they'd cleared the air once and for all.

"We're going to get him, love," he allowed himself the endearment, "but we'll still be here after they've bagged him. And we need to fix what's been broken between us."

A soft sigh escaped her, and Niall watched her swallow before she spoke. The tension that kept her shoulders from sagging left a different kind of ache in his chest, one that he hoped they could make disappear together before he went back to sleep. He blurted out the next words to give her a place to start.

"I hope you're not angry with me anymore, Toni. And I hope you understand that I wasn't keeping secrets to hurt you."

"I know that, Niall," she said at last. "And I know I hurt you, hurt us, by slowing things down after that first time we were together, and then by not telling you everything about my marriage and by keeping the business with Eric quiet for so long. Maybe if I had said something sooner..."

He couldn't let her finish that statement. "We both messed up, Toni. How could you have known who my suspect was if I never told you his name? And why would you have ever wanted to tell me any of the awful things you suspected but couldn't prove against him if it would only dredge up memories you had already banished?"

He lifted his uninjured arm and beckoned for her to come and sit by him on the bed, moving carefully so as not to jar his hurting body. He needed her close, to assure himself that she was whole, that he was well, that they were together, hopefully forever. When he had decided that what he wanted was eternity with her he couldn't say. Maybe the accident had shaken loose all the remaining secrets he'd been keeping from himself about his desires where she was concerned. However it had happened, he accepted it now as gospel.

"I was so scared, Niall." Residual fear kept her admission to a hoarse whisper and it more than echoed his own feelings.

"I know. So was I, though I suspect not for the same reasons as you were."

Puzzled brown eyes turned to look at him. "I don't understand."

She had chosen to sit on his uninjured side, and he reached for her hand, grasping it, and linking their fingers together before he replied.

"These last five months haven't changed that feeling I had the first time I saw you at your friend's birthday party. I still feel like I've been electrocuted, like I'm a walking lightning bolt."

"He changed things," she said bitterly, not responding to his confession. "I was expecting him to send you a bouquet as well before he did anything. I figured you would know what they meant and would be careful going forward. I didn't expect him to be waiting to run you down when you were out jogging."

Niall could hear the horror in her voice, and he wanted to hold her and soothe away the fear. But something tickled in his memory, just out of reach. He tried to bring it into focus, but it stayed just beyond his consciousness, so he let it go and answered her.

"I was so afraid that everything we'd ever said or done with each other had meant nothing when you found out about the surveillance. That I'd been a fool to think what I was feeling was more than just a hard crush, a bad case of lust gone horribly wrong."

He squeezed her fingers, wishing he knew another way to explain his feelings. "I was so afraid I'd lost you, love, and then I woke up and heard you praying. I'm so glad you weren't here to say goodbye. The first time I woke up, you didn't say anything when I called you. I thought that you were a dream."

"I was so scared, Niall," she repeated. "I thought you were dead or in a coma, and I didn't know what to say when you called me. I froze. Like you said, what if it was just a dream, you know?"

Niall turned his head to hers, wincing at the pain, and reached up to pull her face to his. Maybe they weren't all the way back yet, but they both needed the kiss he placed on her lips. No passion, only a promise that he was safe, that they had a chance to make things right, that he wasn't leaving her alone.

"It's not a dream, sweetheart. I'm alive and we're together..."

"Are we, though?" Her question interrupted him. Her eyes slid away from his.

Niall chose his words carefully. This conversation was probably going to be the most important one they'd had so far, and he'd be damned if he sent the wrong message.

"I'd like us to be together in every way, Toni. But we do have to do better this time. We have to be completely open with each other and not keep our questions and assumptions to ourselves. We have to rebuild trust or we're not going to make it. And I can't do this again. Staying away from you was the hardest thing I've ever done."

"It was the worst experience of my life, Niall." Toni's words resonated with him, and he looked down as her eyes overflowed with tears. "Not even when Randy sent me to A&E did I feel as gutted and horrible as I did when you walked away from me that last night. I was so afraid that it was a breakup visit, despite what you told me, because I hadn't said the words back to you. I was so afraid to trust what I felt when I found out about the men keeping tabs on me. I know it's stupid, but I felt like my privacy had been invaded and my options taken away from me again."

A sob escaped her, and she tried to pull away from him, but Niall had had enough. Weariness dragged at him, but he needed her to know that he felt the same way, that he was with her and would be for as long as she wanted him to be.

"If you don't want to break up, then don't run away from me, okay?" He raised her hand to his lips and turned the palm up so he could place a long, tender kiss there. Then he closed her fingers over it and added, "Will you still be here when I wake up again?"

The smile that broke over her face scattered the tears on her cheeks like raindrops in sunshine. She was so exquisite in her grief and in her joy, and the love that had been growing for her since the moment they met burst inside him.

"I won't leave you."

Niall heard everything she hadn't said as he dozed off again holding her hand.

When he woke up the next time, Toni was dozing on the chair next to him. He tried to reach for her hand but couldn't manage it and then the doctor and his parents came in and she woke up with a start. When she saw the others, she stood up at once.

"I'll come back when they're finished, okay? I promise."

He nodded and watched her leave, feeling curiously forlorn. Shaking himself mentally, he accepted his mother's kisses, told his father he was feeling rotten, and bore the doctor's ministrations before everyone settled in for the conversation he knew was about to take place.

He was not surprised at the extent of his injuries. In fact, given what the clear intention had been, he was shocked he didn't have more serious injuries than the ones the doctor mentioned. The van had only clipped his lower body—thank God for incompetent murderers for hire, right?—but enough that in addition to his broken leg, he also had bruised ribs, a broken collar bone, road rash, and concussion from the force with which he'd hit the ground as he dived away from the vehicle. Once he was released, he would need to see the doctor if the headaches didn't ease or he started vomiting, or if he had a fever or dizziness.

He felt dizzy just listening to the man explain what he'd need to do to care for his battered body. He was grateful that his parents were there, and he knew his mother would insist that he go back to the country with them until he was well enough to be on his own. But really, he just wanted Toni, and she wasn't in the room. He drifted off, letting the conversation happen around him, and didn't know when he dozed off again.

When he woke up, Toni was there, reading on her tablet. She looked exhausted and he wondered how much sleep she had gotten since the accident.

"Hi, love!"

His voice was hoarse, and he could do with some water. When she looked up at him, the joy on her face was hard to see without tears welling up. Was this one of the effects of concussion? Because he seemed to have become a weepy mess and he wasn't best pleased about that.

"You're awake!" She smiled at him, shoving the tablet into the big front pocket of the hoodie she was wearing. "Do you need some water?"

He nodded. It was easier than speaking, and he let her raise the head of his bed so he could sip from the plastic cup she held to his lips. After a few sips, he pushed her hand away and she put the cup on the table at his side.

"Do you need anything else?"

"Just a kiss from you," he said, cracking a smile. Literally. "And some lip balm," he added, wincing, "if you have it."

He relaxed when her lips touched his, and then she found the lip balm his mother must have left for him to use and coated his sore lips with it.

"Better?" Her smile was like its own healing potion, warming him inside.

"Much, thanks, love." He reached for her hand before she pulled away. "Sit next to me, please."

She leaned her hip against the bed on his uninjured side and took his hand.

"How does it feel to be wearing a cast and a sling on the same side?"

"So far, so good," he answered. "We'll just have to wait and see what happens when I try to stand up." He chuckled as the first line of a sea shanty about a drunken sailor that he'd learned as a boy in school popped into his head.

"What's so funny?" she asked, looking at him with affection.

Instead of answering her question, he sang the first stanza of the song and Toni laughed with him.

"You'll have to tell me the title so I can listen to it for real," she teased, "because I have no idea how it actually sounds."

Niall let her tease him. They were back, and even if for a while he wouldn't be able to act on the desire he still felt for her—damn his broken body!—it felt good to know that whatever he was feeling, she was feeling it too. He could manage his pain and handle rehab as long as he had her with him for when he forgot that he was a grown man and sulked or whined, as he was sure he'd do. He had never liked being ill, so this was going to be a test of her love for him. Somehow, though, he wasn't worried... he was confident she'd pass with flying colors.

Niall measured his recuperation in milestones. When news came, while he was still at his parents' home, that Randy Richards had been apprehended and was on remand at Belmarsh Prison awaiting his trial, Niall and Toni celebrated with his first trip to the doctor after his hospital stay. And after he was told he was doing well, they stopped for a fruit slushy and sat in the car watching the ducks on the river where they had parked.

"I love slushy dates, don't you?" he asked, licking the melting treat off the side of his large cone.

"I didn't even know that that was a thing," Toni said, chuckling.

"Well, now you know. And as soon as I can eat ice cream again, we're having one of those dates, too."

Toni's laughter made him feel almost giddy with joy. He had her with him and she wasn't going anywhere. When he was cleared to use a crutch to walk instead of being in a wheelchair, they went for a slow amble along the paved path by the river, stopping often so he could rest and feed the water birds. They sat on one of the benches along the bank for a bit to people watch, and Niall smiled at the sweet pleasure of wrapping his woman in his arms, feeling her full body pressed up against him.

His doctor had warned him not to indulge in any activity that would raise his blood pressure until his brain had healed. It had been a month of no sex and only chaste kisses. Niall was beyond ready for their sex date—he had taken to calling every activity they enjoyed together a date—and with his doctor's go ahead, he had planned the perfect return to loving. All he needed was for Toni to show up.

His townhouse had been thoroughly cleaned, the dinner he had asked his mum to help him prepare was waiting to be served, his dad had gifted him a bottle of wine from his private stash, and the gift he had been bought a week earlier was now burning a hole in his trouser pocket. He checked himself one more time, pleased with the way he looked. When the doorbell rang, he took a deep breath and went to open it.

"Hi."

Toni held a beautiful bouquet of deep red roses in a vase. Niall stepped aside to let her in, feeling almost giddy with the rush of lust that hit him as she walked by him, smelling like sex and love and desire and lust. Or maybe it was just his libido roaring into overdrive. He had read somewhere that sometimes a concussion could mess with a man's libido, making it more difficult for him to achieve and sustain an erection. As he followed Toni into his living room, he thanked his lucky stars that he was not one of those guys. If the way his body was lighting up was any indication, he was in the group who saw increased libido. And hallelujah for that!

"I wanted to make another new memory around red roses to expunge the old one. Read the card."

Toni took the card from the flowers, setting the vase down on the coffee table, and handed it to him to read. His eyes grew misty as he read it silently, then aloud.

"I fell in love with this song when I was a teenager. Who knew I would remember it now and realize how it's saying everything I have ever wanted to say to the man of my dreams?"

Niall wished like hell that he could drop to one knee to say what he knew he had to say now and not after dinner like he had planned.

"Come sit with me a minute," he said, pulling her over to sit on the loveseat next to him. "I know that song, and I would sing it for you, but you'd only laugh at me and I need this to be as powerful and romantic as the last few minutes have been."

He watched her eyes widen when he pulled the little ring box from his pocket and opened it.

"I've been in love with you for months, Antonia Larson. And I've known that I'd never find anyone else like you, that you were the one I want to spend the rest of my days with for a long time, too, but I needed to be sure we were on the same page. And now I know we are, I can't think of a better time to ask you the one question I need you to please say yes to. Will you marry me, darling?"

He didn't feel the tear that slid down his cheek, only her thumb wicking it away, her own eyes brimming with tears.

"Yes, Niall. Like the song says, I'll never find another you."

She looked down at the ring in the box. It was a beautiful yellow gold band studded with small diamonds and aquamarines and topped by a gorgeous marquise-cut diamond.

"Do you like it, love?" He hadn't realized he was nervous until that moment.

"It's beautiful, Niall."

She extended her hand, and he pulled the ring from the box and slid it on, loving how the stones lit up against her skin. He raised her hand to his lips and kissed it, letting his mouth linger on the soft skin. And then he kissed his way up to her lips, taking them hungrily.

"It's been too long, love," he whispered against them, nipping the bottom one in a potent tease. "I've been waiting to get you back where you belong."

Toni smiled against his lips. "And where do you think that is?"

"In my arms, in my bed," he growled before kissing her again. "You'd better be ready for me."

"Or what?" Mischief twinkled in her eyes.

"Or you'll get what's coming to you," he threatened, but he was grinning too.

Toni let her hand slip down to the bulge in his trousers and when she squeezed him, he groaned and returned the favor, cupping her breasts and squeezing gently.

"Two can play," he informed her huskily, before he bent his head and pulled her clothed nipple between his teeth.

She rewarded him with a groan of pleasure, and he could feel his temperature rising.

"Darling, I need to feel you. Are you hungry or can we play first?"

For answer, she stood up, extending her newly beringed hand and said, "Ready when you are, love."

And just like that, Niall was a trembling mess of emotions and desires. He followed her, wishing he could ditch the clunky crutch, into his bedroom and let her strip him of his clothes.

"Sit down," she said, and when he did, she continued. "You get to choose how you want this to happen. Do I strip myself and give you a show, or do you do it for me and tease me while you do?"

Ah, decisions, decisions! "Come here," he said.

She could strip for him some other time. Right now, he needed to touch her more than anything else, so when she stood before him, he pulled her clothes off as quickly as he could without popping any of the buttons on her blouse. And then she was lying on his bed, a feast spread out for his enjoyment, and he was kissing her everywhere his mouth could reach. Her breasts were ripe for the sucking, her navel seducing him with its soft pout, her long legs demanding that he push them apart so he could send his fingers into her already wet channel.

"Fuck, darling, you're so ready for me."

She hissed when he teased her opening with his thumb, slicking it so he could slide it over her hard nub. He wanted her sounds, craved them, and every moan and sigh, every gasp and groan ratcheted up his lust until he was leaking precum freely all over himself.

Soft, slow kisses morphed into deep, hungry ones as they tasted and tested and teased each other. Toni tried to jerk his cock but he wasn't interested in his own pleasure just now. He wanted her first release as his fiancée to be memorable.

"Let me please you, darling. I'll get mine soon, but I want this first time to be for you, okay?"

Toni gasped as he plunged a second finger inside her, still rubbing her pleasure button. She gyrated her hips, hissing with every pass of his thumb. Her breathing grew shallower, her words became nonsense, and Niall's heart raced and thundered to the finish with her when she came all over his hand.

"Gorgeous," he whispered, taking another kiss from her panting lips. He raised his hand to his lips and licked his fingers clean, then leaned in to share her taste with her. "Mmm, delicious!"

"Your turn," she whispered when she had recovered and rolled over so she could swallow his leaking cock to the root.

Although Niall was still hampered by the cast on his leg, it didn't stop him from raising his hips to thrust his heated rod up into her willing mouth.

"Toni!" he shouted when she sucked him in again, adding a finger to play at his hole.

Though he had heard of prostate play, he had never had anything or anyone breach his arse before, and now he wanted Toni to do it more than he could express. He didn't even have the brain cells needed to be shocked that he wanted her finger up his hole because the anticipation was going to kill him.

"Do it," he begged her. "Touch me there."

She smiled up at him, rising to her knees and pushing pillows under each of his knees before swirling her fingers in his precum and going back to teasing his hole.

"Mmm. That shouldn't feel so decadent," he groaned. "Push it in, love. Let me feel you."

"I don't want to hurt you," she said, still not breaching him.

"You won't," he promised, gasping when she put the tip of her finger against him and pressed in. "More, love," he begged her. "More."

Toni took her time, sending more of her finger up while she stroked his cock with her other hand. He couldn't think about what it felt like to have an intruding digit in his arsehole, but then she touched something that sent sparks of fire streaking through his body, making his cock jerk hard and his balls tighten. He was going to come from arse play.

"Darling, please," he begged incoherently as she found the magic spot again and teased him. "Please, love, I need ..."

He needed to come, but he needed to feel this sharp and powerful pleasure for as long as his body could bear it.

She stretched out beside him and replaced the hand on his cock with her mouth, sucking him in time with her brushes against his prostate, and he flew!

"Toni!" he screamed as his orgasm roared through him.

She kept finger-fucking his hole and sucking his dick until he was sure he had no more cum to give. His whole body trembled from the most powerful orgasm he'd ever had.

"You're going to have to give me a second to recover, love," he said, his voice hoarse from the shouting.

Toni laughed. "Wishful thinking... I like it!"

He loved it when she teased him. It was a sign of affection and he relished it. He pulled her into his side and kissed her mouth, tasting himself on her tongue.

"Dirty girl," he murmured, licking his way back to her mouth from the hollow of her throat.

"Mmm. I'll take that as a compliment coming from the dirty boy who begged me for it."

She wasn't wrong, he thought as his body succumbed to the power of his climax and he dozed off.

CHAPTER 16

Toni eyed the man sitting next to her surreptitiously as he tapped out whatever it was he was doing on his tablet. Until a few months ago, she hadn't taken a break from work that was more than a weekend long in more than two years, which was also the last time she had seen any man more than once. Feeling threatened by her ex had done a number on her, especially as she suspected that he'd been the one responsible for Eric's untimely demise more than two years ago.

More than once in the last few months, even after they had come to an understanding about how fast they wanted to move in their relationship, she had thought hard about ending things with Niall. She had been so afraid that she'd fall in love with him and that her ex would find a way to end things between them permanently, like he'd done the last time she'd tried to be with someone. She had been right that Eric's death had not been an accident, though she couldn't prove it at the time. Even now, the memory of the bouquet and note that hadn't made sense until after Eric ended up dying in the A&E still frightened her.

A flight attendant's voice crackled over the speaker. "Ladies and gentlemen, as we start our descent, please make sure your seat backs and tray tables are in their full upright position. Make sure your seat belt is securely fastened and all carry-on luggage is stowed underneath the seat in front of you or in the overhead bins. Thank you."

The sound of tray tables being slammed back into place echoed through the cabin. Toni secured her tray table to the seat back in front of her and pushed the small backpack she had carried on with her fully under her seat. Niall looked over at her with a smile.

"Are you okay?"

He knew she hated flying, but she had made it clear that she didn't want him to make a fuss over her for something she considered a weakness. He'd been watchful without mollycoddling her, and she appreciated that he did his best to respect her wishes without losing his own sense of chivalry.

"I'm fine, thank you. Did you finish?"

"Just about. I'll edit it one more time before I send it. But I promise to wait until you're asleep this time."

His grin made her smile. "Thankfully, you don't make a habit of bringing your work with you on dates. It was just that one time."

He smirked, shaking his head at her. "It was, but you weren't best pleased that I'd done that the last time we went away together."

"To be fair, that was also the first time we'd been away together as a couple. A girl expects more than the usual attention the first time," she defended herself.

"I thought I had fulfilled that expectation repeatedly." His brows were doing a seductive dance above amused eyes and his lips twisted in mirth.

"You have a one-track mind, don't you?" she accused him with a long suffering sigh. "You know what I mean."

"Well, I promise you won't see me on this tablet working again for the next week. I'm all yours to do with as you please."

Toni tried not to let his deliberately suggestive words with their seductive promise affect her and failed utterly. However, before she could make an appropriately scathing response, the captain spoke.

"Ladies and gentlemen, we have just been cleared to land at Amsterdam Airport Schiphol. Cabin crew, please take your seats for landing."

When the plane touched down, relief welled inside her. Flying, even short jaunts like this one, was incredibly stressful and Toni could already feel the ache from the tension she'd been carrying in her back and shoulders for the whole trip.

The captain's voice came over the intercom once again, welcoming them to The Netherlands, giving them local time and temperature, and thanking them for flying British Airways. The attendants smiled brightly and wished them a pleasant stay in Amsterdam as they disembarked. They were staying in a cute boutique hotel in the heart of Amsterdam overlooking a canal and by the time they were checked in, Toni was more than ready for a soak in the huge claw-footed tub that she'd glimpsed in the bathroom and her bed.

The suite had a separate bedroom and bathroom, and the living and dining rooms were comfortable enough that they could have Karen and Peter over for dinner at least once. She was excited to see her friend, whom she hadn't seen in a while, and she wanted to catch up on all her news, especially now that she was in a relationship with her Dutch English teacher.

"Shall I order room service for us?" Niall asked her as he deposited their luggage on the floor next to the king-sized bed.

"Nothing too heavy," she replied with a nod. "I'm going to have a bath."

Niall's eyes darkened but he didn't respond, only turned out of the bedroom to place the order. Toni thought he would have asked to join her, and she stifled disappointment that he hadn't. But as she set the water temperature and added some of the luxurious and deliciously scented bath salts to the water, she acknowledged that if Niall was as nervous as she was, he might not feel free to ask.

They'd been together for nine months now, and she was more than relieved that she didn't have to worry about her ex any longer, that thoughts of him would not intrude on what they were building. Niall's work as a security consultant, and his former career in the military, had prepared him to take care of himself when Randy had tried to get rid of him. Niall had healed after the accident, and she reveled in that knowledge.

"The food will be here in an hour." His voice in her ear startled her. "Why aren't you already soaking away the tension? Your shoulders are still up around your ears, baby."

He reached up and squeezed them, making Toni groan. His massages were a delight that she had enjoyed as often as he offered them.

"May I join you? I can get in a quick massage..."

"Yes," she interrupted him. He didn't need to explain or justify his presence in her bath. They were engaged to be married, and though they still lived separate lives in their own spaces back in London, they were committed to making the relationship work until they both decided that it was time to take the next step.

Karen, who had married Peter a couple of months earlier, had been adamant that she shouldn't wait too long to make Niall hers completely. And she knew she would when they got back to England. She would marry the right man this time and she couldn't wait. In the meantime, she knew what would make her completely boneless and she wanted him to be the one to suggest that activity. Still, she was tired, and maybe he was, as well.

"Or," he lowered his lips until they were brushing her earlobe, "I could relax the whole of you another way."

His tone was openly seductive, and his breath was warm on her skin, paradoxically making her shiver with awareness. She arched her neck, giving him room to plant soft kisses and nips along its length.

"Your perfume is so sexy," he whispered, "it makes me want to ravish you."

Toni smiled, though her heart was racing. Why was it that even now, after all these months together, even as they were discovering each other's sexual preferences, she still felt like everything with him was a first?

"I'm all for whatever you feel like doing, as long as it includes me in bed."

Almost as soon as the words left her lips, she gasped, realizing how what she had said could be misinterpreted. She really had only meant to say she wanted to go to bed to sleep, not that she wanted to make love. She did, but that wasn't... she halted the train of thought, especially since the person who needed to hear it was not privy to it.

"Water's ready."

Toni shook her head at herself. She'd been so caught up in her head, in thoughts of what Niall might do to her in the tub, that she'd forgotten she was filling it to take a bath.

"Thank you." She smiled at him.

Conscious of his eyes on her and feeling the usual diffidence—she was on the wrong side of thirty-five and she feared her body would show it—she stripped out of the rest of her clothes and stepped into the tub which was three quarters of the way full. Niall stepped in behind her and pulled her down in front of him, reaching around her belly to pull her closer. They'd never taken a bath together before, only managing to shower together a few times, some of them being a hurried affair before Niall had to leave for work.

The intimacy of the situation swelled around them as Niall swept water over her shoulders and her breasts, as he leaned in to suckle her neck, as he squeezed her shoulder blades and rubbed the tight muscles in her neck and down her spine.

"Mmm, thank you. This is just what I need."

She wanted to sound her gratitude before words became impossible, as they no doubt would if his straying hands had anything to do with it. He kneaded her shoulder blades and pushed and rolled the tight muscles there. Pressing his fingers into the muscles down her back, he slid his hands around to her belly, sliding them up until his fingers encircled her nipples. He pinched them, just hard enough to make her body tighten with pleasure.

When he turned her head to the side so he could kiss her, she relaxed completely against his chest, inhaling deeply between his kisses.

"Open your legs, Toni," he demanded hoarsely.

When she did as he asked, spreading them as wide apart as she could in the tub, he swept a finger over her hard nub, teasing it with barely there touches, all the while kissing her senseless.

"You like?" he whispered against her lips.

When she nodded, he smiled and rubbed harder, making her gasp. Her tired muscles softened further until she was loose from the pleasure he had unleashed in her. She writhed as he worked her, sliding first one finger, then a second inside her. Her moans grew louder as he pushed her higher and just when she thought she couldn't bear to hold back any longer, he pulled his fingers from her.

"Turn around, baby," he demanded hoarsely, helping her to comply with his order. Water threatened to spill over the side of the tub as she straddled his lap, her knees jutting out of the water, but she didn't care.

Then he kissed her again, this time letting his big hands roam from her shoulders down her back to her hips and buttocks. He squeezed the high, round cheeks, dragging a moan from her. She wanted him as desperately as she had the first time they'd fallen into bed together. Only this time, her mind and heart were in sync. She knew what she wanted with him. Drunk with desire, she sought his mouth for another searing kiss, her whole body tight with a different tension this time, needing him to fill her up so she could fall apart.

He helped her raise her bottom so he could slide his length inside her and then he helped her to ride him. It didn't take long. A few slaps of her bottom against his thighs as he worked her clit and she was coming all over him. She grunted as she came, collapsing against his chest, utterly weak and completely relaxed. Niall shifted her off his cock, seizing her lips in a brutal kiss before he jacked himself off in three hard pulls, growling out his release between clenched teeth.

His seed splashed onto her belly and the sides of her thighs before sliding into the water. Toni watched mesmerized as it pooled between them. Then Niall stood up, displacing the bath water, and lifted her to stand with him.

"Let's rinse off. The food will be here soon."

He held her hand while she stepped out of the tub, then turned and pulled the plug before stepping out himself. She set the water temperature for the shower, her legs still shaky from her orgasm, and let him lead her in and wash her off gently.

"Dry off and go get ready for bed. I'll be out in a jiffy."

When he walked back into the bedroom, Toni was sitting in the armchair, her legs curled under her, wrapped in a blanket she'd pulled from the bed. Niall pulled sweats and a t-shirt from his suitcase and dropped the towel to change, making her mouth water at the sight of him. She was too tired to go another round just yet, but the sight of his body made her wish she was ready again.

"If what you're telegraphing with that look is true, you'll have to give me a few minutes to recover," he teased, interrupting her perving.

"I can't help it if you look like a model, can I? I mean, how long have you been out of the military now? Is it even right for you to look so damn ripped all the time?"

Niall laughed. "Sorry not sorry." He went to crouch next to her. "Do you want to eat in here?"

"No. I'll come out. I was just waiting for you."

He stood and pulled her to her feet, leading her out to the sitting area where she immediately curled up again on the sofa. A knock sounded and he went to let the server in. Once the tray was situated, Niall tipped the young woman and closed the door. Toni watched as he removed the cloches covering the food and turned back to her.

"So, I went a somewhat heart-healthier route tonight and ordered veggie burgers and tuna sandwiches. Which would you like? They come with French fries, and there's wine, coffee, and chocolate cake for dessert."

"Why did it take them an hour to put this together?" What he'd ordered shouldn't have taken more than half an hour.

Niall waggled his eyebrows mischievously. "I told them we wouldn't be ready for an hour."

Toni chuckled. "You're just too much, you know that?"

"Apparently not for you," he answered with a grin. "So, what do you want?"

"I'll have a burger, please, and some fries."

She loved how he always waited on her, no matter where they were. She had given up trying to make him change his ways soon after they got together because he'd adamantly refused to be anyone but who he was. In his family, the men served their women. She'd seen it the first time she'd visited his parents' home, so she knew it wasn't a fluke.

He handed her the plate with her food and a napkin and while she sorted herself out, freeing her arms from the confines of the blanket so she could eat unimpeded, he made his own plate and poured two glasses of wine.

"Eat up. You'll need your strength."

She shook her head at his teasing smile, but she dug in, enjoying how deliciously seasoned the burger was. Although she wasn't vegetarian, she had discovered a love for well-made veggie burgers, and she was glad this one didn't disappoint. And she loved that Niall seemed to remember everything she said she liked and that he tried to give them to her when he could.

She recalled how worried she'd been when she realized that she was in love with him because she hadn't been sure it was love. But now she knew that what she was feeling was the real deal. She had been so worried because she didn't know how she would handle it if anything were to happen to him because of her. She had been so frightened when he'd been hit, especially because this time, the man she was with meant more to her than Eric had.

"What's got you frowning so fiercely, love?"

Niall's question brought her out of her musing. "Just thinking about the last time I was with someone for more than one date."

"Not sure I like the idea of you thinking about some other man when you're with me, love."

He sounded amused, but Toni looked at him quickly anyway, just to make sure he wasn't serious and trying to pass it off as unimportant.

"I wasn't thinking about him, per se, just about my dating in general. I never really believed I'd ever find someone again. I definitely wasn't prepared for you."

She cocked a brow at him, and he waggled his own. "The best things in life are unexpected," he declared.

She smiled at him, and they finished their meal in silence after that. Her eye caught the glint of the ring on her finger and her heart swelled up with love and pride and joy. She had called Karen the day after she had said yes, and they'd squealed on the phone like teenagers. It would be good to see her friend again, especially as she now resided in The Netherlands with her husband.

She had chosen to start this holiday where Karen lived so they could plan her wedding together and decide on where she should ask Niall to take her. He had said it was up to her, that he would go wherever she chose. She had a few ideas and so did her friend. They would compare notes and try to whittle down the list to two. Who knew? Maybe Niall would take her to both places. A girl could dream.

The days flew by. Between them, she and Karen chose Paris and Florence. Niall could decide, once they were back home, which one he wanted to go with. They took in a show with Peter and Karen, visited all the touristy spots in Amsterdam, took an Amsterdam canal tour, and lazed about in bed, making love and sleeping. They had both needed the holiday, and she had been happy to see Niall keep his promise not to let his job intrude on their time together.

Their visit to her parents, while it was less eventful than the trip to Amsterdam, was no less engaging. Once the hugging and handshakes were over, Mr. Larson got right down to the nitty gritty.

"I hear that we have you to thank in part for helping our girl get her life back completely," he said. "Please accept my wife's and my sincerest thanks."

Her father always got very stiff and formal when he was feeling emotional. Niall accepted his thanks and then her mother said, "So when's the wedding?"

They had been overjoyed to hear of her engagement, though her father hadn't been able to help reminding her that they had yet to meet the man and imploring her not to make the same mistake twice. So, though she knew Niall was the right man, she would let them have their say. This time, she was doing what she wanted with the certain knowledge that she was doing the right thing for the right reason.

"We haven't decided yet," she replied.

"But you and my parents will be the first to know once we figure it out," Niall added.

Toni's heart warmed with love. He had been so nervous about meeting them, although he'd done his best to hide that from her. And yet here he was, trying to make sure things stayed good between her and her parents. She shot him an approving glance and he smiled in return.

"Are you planning to have a big ceremony or something small and tasteful?"

The question made it clear what her mother wanted, but again they hadn't thought about it and she refused to be forced into doing what others wanted. While she didn't plan on repeating the mistakes of her first wedding, she was an adult and she could plan whatever she wanted without assistance from anyone, thank you very much!

"Not that I mean to intrude, but where will you be living after you marry?"

Toni watched as Niall hid a snicker in a cough. He was not helping by finding her mother amusing instead of annoying, which is what she was being just then.

"Mum, we haven't done anything more than get engaged so far. We both work challenging jobs and there isn't always time for these discussions. But," she hurried to add, "we've got time. There's no rush."

Niall gave her a funny look that she didn't understand until they were on their way back to London. He turned to glance at her before saying,

"There is no rush? Is that what you really want, love? Are we going too fast for you?"

"I only said that to shut her up, Niall. She was getting more and more intrusive with the questions, and I was tired of it."

"Maybe we should talk about these things and settle them so the next time we'll have answers for them."

Not a bad idea. "Can we do this tomorrow over lunch? I'm too tired to think about all that now." She reached over and rested her hand on his thigh for a moment. "Thanks for putting up with my parents' antics today. They can be a handful sometimes."

"They love you, and that's really all that matters to me. Your dad is still trying to figure me out to see if I'm good for his baby girl, but I can't say I blame him."

"Next time we go up, I'll make sure my brothers are with us. They behave when the boys are around."

The talk about the wedding was brief. They both wanted it simple and intimate, they both wanted to do both Florence and Paris, and they both wanted to move to a less urban area, even if their commute ended up being longer.

And on the morning of her wedding, Toni stood in front of her best friend, who was dressed in a pale blue tea-length dress, trying to quell the butterflies. It had been a long road to this point, and there had been a lot of hurt and sadness. She had been broken... and then Niall came in like a white knight and gave her a new reason to hope. She had found her way back to love with a most unexpected man and she would never look back again.

"This dress is beautiful, Toni," Karen said, doing up the last of the cloth-covered buttons that closed up the back of the lace-covered cream satin dress. It was a long-sleeved vintage frock, elegant and stylish, with a gauzy train flowing from the accompanying headpiece.

"It is, and I'm so glad I got it for a steal."

"You are a beautiful bride, Toni. Niall won't know what hit him when he sees you in this."

Resisting the urge to touch her intricately styled hair, she turned and looked at the back of the dress in the mirror. It was beautiful and she was glad she had ignored her mother and bought it when it went on sale. A knock was followed almost immediately by it opening and Niall sticking his head in.

"You do know you're breaking one of the cardinal rules of a wedding, don't you?" she asked, smirking, while Karen laughed outright.

"And in ten minutes we'll be breaking another one when we walk each other down the aisle behind our parents and siblings. Are you ready?"

"I am. Are you?"

He stepped into the room and twirled for her to see. He was wearing a cream-colored tux to match her dress with a blue bow tie and vest to match the women in the wedding party.

"I look forward to popping every button on this gorgeous dress later," he announced before stepping out and closing the door behind him.

Karen's eyes widened. "He wouldn't... would he?"

Toni laughed. "He would."

Hours later, after the "I do's" and the vows, after the speeches and the cake, after the bouquet and the garter toss and the dancing, when they were alone in the honeymoon suite of the hotel where the wedding had been held, Niall kept his word.

"I promise to find every one of the buttons and pay for them to be re-attached, darling," he murmured as he bathed her shoulders in kisses. "But I am a man of my word. How would it have looked if I hadn't done as I promised?"

Toni laughed and wrapped her arms around his neck. "I love a man I can trust to do what he says he'll do."

"Yes, you do, you lucky thing!" he sassed her, then undressed them both.

Toni kissed him to shut him up, but he didn't seem to care. Lucky man... he got the girl, after all.

THE END

AUTHOR

KT Bond is an emerging author of contemporary romance across many sub-genres. She started her second career as a ghostwriter of sweet and erotic romances upon her retirement from public education almost seven years ago, giving her clients the love stories that they wanted. Now she writes stories for her own readers, using that experience to show her the way forward. She knows that every life has a tale waiting to be told, and it is her honor and privilege to share the joy of love with you, one story at a time.

KT is a retired English teacher, an avid reader, a new Nana, the chief cook and dog walker in her family. She is a member of the Romance Writers of America. This is the second book in the *Serendipity* series, and KT's ninth book in her own name.

SOCIAL MEDIA

https://linktr.ee/kdjb

COMING NEXT

Back to Last: Serendipity, Book 3

Chrissy and Rory must decide whether or not they can handle the on-again, off-again affair they have been having since her thirtieth birthday party, which is where they met. Can the feelings they clearly have for each other finally outlast Rory's fear of commitment?

4 Horsemen Publications

Romance

Ann Shepphird
The War Council

Emily Bunney
All or Nothing
All the Way
All Night Long: Novella
All She Needs
Having it All
All at Once
All Together
All for Her

KT Bond
Back to Life
Back to Love
Back at Last

Lynn Chantale
The Baker's Touch
Blind Secrets
Broken Lens

Mandy Fate
Love Me, Goaltender
Captain of My Heart

Mimi Francis
Private Lives
Private Protection
Run Away Home
The Professor

4HorsemenPublications.com